SMOKE AND MIRRORS

Harem of Freaks Book 3

CRYSTAL ASH

PROLOGUE

Pacing back and forth in a cage is no way to live.

I could feel my muscles weakening, my mind going insane.

My rage went past the point of boiling over, but there was nothing left for me to do behind these steel bars. I gnawed at them until the humans electrocuted me, then sedated me again. Once, I was one of the most powerful predators on earth, but in here I was powerless.

The best I could do was disfigure someone if they got close enough, but it had been five long years since I've felt the satisfaction of sinking my teeth into a weaker animal's throat.

Every moment I was conscious, I fantasized about killing them all and claiming my victory, of taking ownership of my freedom to claim my mate, who I've yet to meet. I felt her out there, despite having never seen her face. What would she think if she saw me like this? I needed to be more than a caged pet to win her heart.

If Mamma were still alive, I knew she'd be ashamed of

me for not only the things I've done, but for feeling this way.

"Always practice *ahimsa*, my son," she told me. "Even when we feed, we must not cause unnecessary harm. When the urge to destroy consumes you, that is when *ahimsa* is most important."

Well, I had certainly done minimal harm in my time here, although that was more out of circumstance than choice. I hadn't ripped anyone's throat out simply because I didn't have the reach, nor the strength, anymore. Maybe that displeased Lord Shiva, but I'd been in captivity here for so long, I since gave up hope of having my prayers answered.

And so I paced back and forth like the swinging pendulum in a clock. I agitated the humans in hopes that one of them would finally put me out of my misery. When knocked out, I dreamed of my mate. I felt the comfort of her presence, even though I have no idea who she is.

She's the only shred of hope I had left.

MELODY

I thought it was the heavy weight of despair in my chest as I woke up, but it turned out to be just Connor's arm.

He snored softly next to me as I slid out from under him and stretched. My pointed toes and outstretched arms above my head touched the fake wood paneling before I could truly get a good stretch in. Such was the reality of living in a trailer.

Sure, having an actual house sounded nice, but to be honest, I had no idea what that was like. I spent my whole life in a trailer, so traveling in one as a carnival performer wasn't much of an adjustment at all.

I shifted to a diagonal angle, stretching my legs over Connor's hips to maximize my stretch before relaxing. With a yawn and rub of my eyes, I tried to recall last night's dream.

They were different every night now and only growing more vivid. Sometimes I was running on four paws, howling at the moon. Other times I was in the dark, eerie silence of the ocean, using echolocation to navigate my way around. Sometimes I flew across cities and the most breathtaking natural landscapes. I could never see exactly what I was. All I knew while flying was that I was bigger than a bird. I wondered if Razvan experienced the same views.

No, don't think about Razvan, I scolded myself harshly.

It pained me to not think fondly of the tattooed, enigmatic dragon shifter. I thought I could read people, but he fooled me so well. I couldn't help but see the good in everyone, and I thought I saw a side of him he didn't reveal to anyone else. I even thought a unique connection sparked between us.

But he proved to be exactly the man I initially perceived him to be—an expert game player and heartbreaker. He kissed me onstage in front of everyone while his girlfriend watched from backstage. Connor saw it too, but genuinely didn't seem to mind. If anything, he encouraged me to talk to Raz again. But that deliberate deception was not something I wanted in my life, especially if I was going to entertain the idea of dating multiple men.

Last night's dream was different, though. They caged me in a different carnival, an especially bad one where the staff did little to hide their exploitation of animals. I could smell fear, death, and despair through my heightened senses. Power, strength and incomprehensible anger flowed through me, but I had no outlet to express it. All I could do was pace back and forth in a small cage.

I never felt such bleak hopelessness like that before. Not even back home in my shitty trailer park life before joining the carnival. When Connor and I saw how Hunter was mistreated back in Drowningville, I thought nothing could top that kind of sorrow. When Razvan told me he was sold into a circus by his own family, that opened the fresh wound all over again.

But that was nothing like this. This dream no longer made me an outside observer. I felt it. I *knew* what it was like to be caged, tortured, and forced to entertain. It consumed me so much that I didn't even notice when Connor stirred next to me until he pulled me back into his embrace.

"Mornin', babe," he drawled, kissing my neck lazily.

"Mornin', handsome." What was it about mornings that made us sound extra southern?

I snuggled into his heat, his warmth and protection. All I wanted to do was shake off the all-consuming sadness and despair of that dream and soak into how good he made me feel.

"How're you feeling today?" I kissed the hollow of his throat.

"Sore," he groaned. "So fuckin' glad we're not onstage today."

I hesitated before saying what was on my mind. "You should probably stay off your prosthetics today."

"Yes, babe, I know," he sighed.

"You know I'm honestly not trying to nag you." I swirled my fingertips in the soft chest hair just below his throat. "I just hate seeing you in pain."

"Pain is inevitable," he grunted, rolling onto his back and pulling me with him so I splayed across his chest.

I lowered my head to listen to the watery thud of his heartbeat, my fingers tracing the Marine Corps emblem tattooed on the other side of his chest. "It can be avoided if you take the time to rest."

"Rest is worse than physical pain for someone like me," he said with a throaty chuckle. "Doing nothing will make me even more insane than I already am."

I opened my mouth to tell him he wasn't insane and promptly shut it, knowing it would be of no use to argue. Connor dealt with his PTSD and loss of his legs through self-deprecating humor. He didn't do it for sympathy. I was beginning to see it helped him to make light of his situation.

So instead I complained, "Why do you always have to argue with me?"

He propped his head up with one arm and brushed a kiss along my eyelids. "You're so damn beautiful in the morning." With his other arm wrapped around me, he promptly slapped my ass. "See, babe? No argument here."

"Changing the subject doesn't count," I pouted.

Laughing, he shifted his broad, muscular body out from under me. I loved watching him move up close. The muscles under his skin were like a landscape of shifting sands—rising and falling, solid and rippling.

He laid on his side, facing me on the same pillow. His green eyes swallowed me up like the deepest, darkest forest.

"I'll go nuts if I don't walk around at least a little, but I promise I'll take it easy, babe."

I sighed, knowing that was the best I was going to get from my stubborn ex-Marine. "Thank you. For *almost* listening to me."

"You're lucky I love you," he chuckled, dropping a light kiss to my nose before pushing himself up to rise from bed.

"Hey." I grabbed his arm, stopping him from leaving

the bed, and pulled him back to me. "You know I really am lucky to have you, right?" My mouth found his to pull a long, lingering kiss from him, morning breath be damned. "And I love you too."

Up close, I could see the conflict in his forest green eyes. Struggle and conflict ruled this man's world in ways that were unimaginable to most people. He lost so much, and not just the physical parts of him. I wanted to remind him every day that he would always be worthy of love, especially when he didn't believe it himself.

"You're so sweet to me, babe," he murmured, resting his forehead on mine. It wasn't a full acceptance of it yet, nor a total brush-off. He was trying, and that was all I could ask for.

A soft *tap-tap-tap* on the trailer door broke through our intimate moment.

"Whaaaat?" Connor groaned at the intrusion.

"Um, you guys up?"

My heart lifted in my chest when I recognized the voice of the handsome wolf shifter. Hunter!

"Only if your furry ass has coffee and bacon," Connor answered.

I stifled a giggle. He was always so grumpy in the morning, it was actually adorable at this point.

"Well, I got one of the two. Just thought I'd share."

"We'll be right out, Hunter!" I called out, pulling the sheet back and reaching to the floor for my clothes.

"Oh, *now* you want to get out of bed."

Connor's smirk told me he was teasing. He and Hunter got to be good friends in the past week. Not to mention he practically threw me at the gorgeous wolf shifter whenever we were together.

"Don't tell me you don't want any of his bacon," I said with a kiss as I stepped into my shorts. "Or his coffee, whichever he has."

"The first one!" Hunter called.

"Mmm, bacon," Connor crooned as he pulled on a shirt.

The three of us seemed to have a unique bond ever since we rescued the wolf shifter and his two children from the especially sadistic carnival in Drowningville. In exchange for saving his life, he volunteered to perform a half-shifted Wolf Man act, which earned our new ragtag team of sideshow performers some serious local buzz. Each show became bigger and more crowded than the last, and they only wanted more.

However, back-to-back nightly shows took their toll on us performers. Connor was putting so much pressure on his legs during his acrobatic stilt walking, he had intense pain the last couple of nights. Thankfully, the weekend finished and Nigel, the carnival manager, gave us the next night off. A different program would go on during the slower weekday nights.

When we were decent, I opened the trailer door and tried not to smile too brightly at the beautiful pale man with golden eyes. His platinum, shoulder-length hair was wavy this morning, probably an effect of the lovely midsummer humidity. He was dressed simply in a gray T-shirt and dark jeans but still managed to look like a model with otherworldly beauty.

"Hey, Hunt." I bit my tongue, cringing at how I shortened his name, but it was too late to take back now.

"Mornin', Mel," he greeted me with an easygoing smile

as his gaze flickered downward shyly. "You look nice today."

"Ahaha, seriously? I literally just rolled out of bed." My heart fluttered like butterfly wings in my chest. "But thanks. You look nice too." Sweet baby Jesus, why did he have to be so pretty *and* polite?

"What's this about bacon?" Connor called from behind me.

"I have some." Hunter nodded to the bundle of butcher paper he held at his side. "Me and the kids took down a boar the other night. I'm telling you, Con, this is the most delicious bacon I've ever had in my life."

"Well, get a fire goin' and put the griddle on, boy!" He slapped my ass and hoisted himself onto the kitchen counter to start a pot of coffee, ignoring my glare in the process.

Hunter tried to politely look away, but I still caught his lip bite as he tried to hold back a laugh.

"Oh, don't get all shy, Hunt. I've seen you naked." Why embarrass just myself when I could embarrass him too?

"Yes, you have." His lips pulled back into a sultry smile. Damn it. I did not embarrass him at all. Not that he had any reason to be—he looked exquisite with or without clothes on. Lithe muscles covered his tall frame, and yes, *it* was very nice to look at as well. Even though I only got a quick glance because it was right after he shifted from Wolf Man to human. I hugged him after our first show together, not realizing he needed to be naked in order to shift.

It was beyond awkward at the time, but now that it occurred in hindsight I didn't mind bringing it up for flirty banter. And apparently Hunter didn't mind either.

We got the fire started, and I carefully set up the cast iron griddle over the flames, held up by two cinder blocks.

"Where are the kids this morning?" I asked.

"Sleeping in," he said, laying thick strips of bacon onto the hot pan. "It was a challenging hunt for them, but they did so well." His eyes beamed with pride and predatory instinct. "They need challenges like that to grow into strong wolves."

Another question weighed on my mind, which he seemed to sense. When he finished laying the strips of bacon, he folded up the butcher paper and moved to sit next to me. The side of his body brushed mine in a clearly intentional move.

"What if that boar was a shifter?" I said in a low voice, watching the strips of meat sizzle. "Can you tell?"

"Yes," he said, putting a hand on my knee reassuringly. He was getting bolder with touching me lately and my insides did backflips. "We can smell if another animal is also human. Most shifters can sense it in some way."

I blew out a breath. "That makes me feel better."

"It is interesting to think about," he mused. "Why other animals are okay to kill but humans are not."

"Some humans should absolutely be killed," I spat with more venom than I intended. "Like the ones who captured and tortured you. Predators like Syko. And the ones who've hurt Connor so badly."

My mind drifted to the ex-fiancee who left him, and the woman sending him messages on his phone. I still hadn't brought that up. Every time I thought about it, I felt immature and stupid to be jealous. She had him before he was injured, then discarded him. The text asked, "Are you ever going to talk to me again?" which indicated he wasn't talking to whoever she was.

And regardless, I had no legs to stand on. He was encouraging me to be with other guys. What right did I have to get upset over a text?

Hunter picked up a pair of tongs and began flipping the bacon over. "I agree with you, Mel. But there are laws that protect humans and not other animals." He ran a hand through his silky hair that could've landed him on a shampoo commercial. "And predators like me prey on other animals to live. It's not that simple."

"Yeah," I agreed, still hypnotized by his hair.

"BABE!" Connor yelled from inside the trailer. "Come get coffee!"

"Yes, sir," I said sarcastically as I jumped the two steps to get inside.

"Hmm, I like it when you call me sir." He grabbed my waist and pulled me to stand between his muscular thighs for a kiss. While sitting on the counter, he was taller than me by several inches and seemed to enjoy the perspective.

"Well?" he inquired when our lips broke apart.

"Well, what?"

A naughty grin followed. "Has he asked you out yet?"

2

MELODY

I blinked. "Excuse me?"

"Ah, guess he hasn't. Shy fucker needs to step it up." Connor grinned as he pushed three mugs of piping hot coffee into my hands.

"Wait, are you and him like, planning this behind my back?"

"I prefer the term 'surprising you'. Maybe 'sweeping you off your feet'." He dropped a light kiss to my nose. "Just a date, babe, not a big deal. For you to get to know each other."

"Okay, but..." I struggled to put words to my feelings. "It's kind of weird that my boyfriend is also playing matchmaker."

"He makes you happy," he said matter-of-factly. "You light up like a goddamn Christmas tree every time you see him."

"Yes, but so do y—"

"I know I do, babe. This isn't about me, though." He took back the coffee mugs, set them down, and placed my hand over his heart. "I have you. I know that, and I'm secure in that fact. That guy," he jerked his chin out toward Hunter, "is a good dude. I'm comfortable calling him my friend and I want him to be happy too. If you're feeling him and he feels the same, he deserves to feel what I do when I wake up next to you. He's suffered so much, he deserves to taste a kiss like yours, babe."

"Goddamnit, Connor." I yanked my hand away from his chest to quickly wipe the tears building in my eyes. "You going from grumpy as hell to all sappy and sweet gives me whiplash sometimes."

"I'm here to keep you on your toes," he smirked with an affectionate final swat to my ass. Thrusting the coffee mugs into my hands once again, he added, "Just wait 'til I get you to make up with Raz."

"No." I froze, all humor and smile gone from my face. "Don't talk to me about him again. That's over and I mean it."

"It never had a chance to begin," he retorted before waving toward the door. "Let's move, babe. I don't want to eat no cold-ass bacon."

Clutching the three coffees for dear life, I held the door open with my back to allow Connor outside. Even without his prosthetic legs, his movements were swift and as natural to him as breathing. Once he was off the bottom step and on the ground outside, he pressed into the ground to lift his hips and thighs up, then walked *on his hands* to the log where Hunter was sitting. His butt and legs never touched the ground.

"Jesus, Connor. Making us look like shit," Hunter joked.

"It's all in the core, man. Thanks, babe," he said as I distributed coffee cups.

"So what you're saying is I should be doing sit-ups every day. Thank you, Mel." Hunter's smile made me melt a little as his hand brushed mine.

"Nah, sit-ups are pretty ineffective, to be honest. They only target your upper abs. You gotta do planks, leg lifts, and variations of those to hit your obliques too. But hey," he slapped Hunter on the back, "keep bringin' home the bacon, boy, and I'll keep sayin' you're in perfect shape."

"Trying to get in my pants, Con?" Hunter grinned.

"Keep on feeding me and I'll do anything you want," came the reply. "Maybe I'll even show Mel how certain things are done."

"Excuse me?!" I cried. "I didn't hear you complaining last night!"

"Kidding, babe." He blew a kiss in my direction, which I pretended to brush off.

The guys continued their bantering while I curled up with my coffee and crispy strips of bacon. It *was* really good. Flavorful with just enough fat and lean meat.

I chewed, savoring the taste while I listened to the guys talk with only half an ear. Not really paying attention to what they talked about, I just enjoyed hearing their voices.

They talked and interacted as if they'd been friends for years. Normally so wary and closed off, Connor's body language was relaxed and open. Hunter, too, had been extremely cautious at first. He only watched me for a few days at first because he didn't want to scare me with what he was, even though I never feared him, not even when he was howling and roaring in his cage before we rescued him.

While quieter and more soft-spoken than Connor, Hunter laughed genuinely as he sat back, listening to Connor's stories and antics. It warmed my heart to know he trusted us and wanted to hang around, despite the fact that we were in the same business that captured, tortured, and drugged not only him but his children.

Connor was in this business because of necessity. If he didn't perform, he would be another homeless, disabled veteran on the street. Me? The carnival was my only happy memory as a child, but my first night onstage proved to be a nightmare. It was only because of desperation for money that I stuck with it, lest I be homeless myself.

Only because of Connor's strict but encouraging coaching did I discover my love to perform. Nothing was as thrilling as walking onstage and commanding a crowd. By some kind of miracle, I became ringmistress when we ended up here in Crying Falls. I still couldn't believe we were selling out tickets. Connor, Razvan, and Hunter were all brilliant of course. I just hoped to do them justice by hyping them up well enough.

And still I couldn't ignore the fact that shifters were being captured and forced to perform as exotic freaks. It sickened me and did more than shatter my dream of the carnival as a happy escape from my home life. Hunter and Razvan were just the two that happened to be in this area. How many more could there be?

My dream returned to the forefront of my mind like a punch to the stomach. I was an animal behind bars. Predatory rage flowed through me like an overdose of adrenaline. I never wanted to kill someone so badly in my life.

But what stood out the most right then was the Ferris wheel peeking out over tops of tents.

I wrapped my hands around my coffee cup and closed my eyes, trying hard to grasp any more details of that place, but they were already fleeting as dreams tend to be. I was so deep in my own mind, I didn't even realize Hunter came to sit beside me until I heard his soft, "Hey."

"Oh, shit!" I shrieked, nearly jumping out of my skin. "Hey!"

"Didn't mean to scare you," he laughed softly.

"You didn't. I was just... thinking about something," I said lamely, then looked over to where the guys were sitting before. "Where'd Con run off too?"

"Said he had to take a shit, so he'd be a few minutes or thirty," he smirked.

"Of course," I groaned.

Hunter's gaze dropped to the ground. He licked his lips, an act I wished my mind could record and play it back slowly.

He cleared his throat. "So hey Mel," he began, lacing his fingers and then undoing the motion. Then his hands closed into fists.

Oh god, he's nervous, I realized. I found it endearing and utterly adorable.

"Do you want to check out the carnival together?" he asked with a lopsided smile. "You know, like normal people."

"Just you and me?" I blurted out. Even though Connor told me this was coming, it did nothing to stop that rush of jittery nerves and pure glee when a crush asked you out. My pulse jumped to a racing beat while my stomach made victorious flips.

"Yeah, if that's cool with you." He swallowed. "Connor can come t—"

"No no, that's okay." I placed a hand on his forearm to reassure him. "I'd love to. Just you and me is totally cool. I'd, um," dare I say it? "I'd love to get to know you better."

His shy smile broke into a full-out grin. "Me too, Mel. And seriously, like," he ran a hand through his hair again and how the fuck was I supposed to resist him when he did that? "Absolutely no pressure or anything. We can just eat horrible food and shoot wooden ducks or whatever. I know you're with Con and this whole situation is just kind of weird."

"I know you two have been talking," I said. "And it is weird, but so far, I'm feeling okay with it as long as you two are."

"The feeling is mutual," he replied, his shoulders sagging like a weight was off them. "And if this makes things harder for you two, just say the word and I'll back off. You two are my friends first and I don't want to hurt either of you."

"I appreciate that," I said sincerely, even though I felt in my heart it would never be an issue. Hunter was on the short list of people that Connor trusted.

The thoughts weighing heavily on my mind were the ones I was still too scared to ask. Like, what would we tell his kids if things went really well between us? And before Hunter spoke to me and Connor, I had dreams about him much like the one I had last night. I still had no idea how to tell him or even if I should.

Even more, I was scared of what those dreams actually meant. I wasn't a shifter, I knew that. Both Hunter and Razvan said I smelled human, but slightly different. I had a strong suspicion both bits of information were connected, but how?

"Want me to come get you when the carnival opens?" Hunter asked, oblivious to my internal conflict.

"Sure!" I beamed at him. "It'll be less crowded that early."

"My thoughts exactly," he grinned as he rose to his feet. "See you in a bit, Mel."

"See you," I said, looking up at him dreamily. "Oh, and thanks for the bacon!"

"Any time." He paused, lingering as if he wanted to say or do something else, but then kept on moving. "Tell Connor I said bye."

"Will do."

I watched him walk away on his tall, lean frame toward the woods. Only when he was behind the dense brush did I catch a glimpse of his platinum hair turning into snowy white fur.

I curled back up in my chair, unable to keep the ridiculous grin off my face. I had a date with a sexy wolf shifter today!

3

MELODY

"You nervous?" Connor teased.

I checked my mascara in the mirror again, stepped back, and straightened out my clothes.

"A little," I admitted. "I've never been on a real date before."

"Seriously?" he stared at me in disbelief. "If I'da known that, I would have wined and dined you way sooner."

"You still can." I flashed a smile at him over my shoulder. "After we get your new prosthetics. Those are more important."

"Fuck that," he grumbled, sliding his hands around my waist as he pressed a sensual kiss to the back of my neck. "You're more important."

"I like you healthy and not in pain," I informed him. "You're less grumpy that way."

"I always find a reason to be grumpy," he chuckled with a playful swat to my ass. "And I need a miracle to afford new legs, anyway. I'm definitely not waiting that long to make my girl feel special."

"You already make me feel special." I spun in his arms and kissed him deeply, not caring that I'd have to reapply my lipstick. With my hands wrapped around his strong neck, my lips and tongue told him without words exactly how I felt.

We parted breathlessly, pausing for half a beat.

"And if a miracle is what we need, then we'll make it happen." With that, I turned back to the mirror and popped open my lipstick tube.

"Ah, to be eighteen and full of hope again," he laughed. My age was his favorite jab at me whenever I tried being positive.

"You never know," I said, carefully applying the red pigment to my lips. "We did find people who can turn into animals after all."

Right on cue, three raps came to the trailer door and my heart jumped into my throat.

"Sup, Hunter. She'll be right out," Connor greeted.

With a final check over myself as they small-talked, I swallowed my nerves and left the bathroom. *Why am I so nervous, anyway?* I wondered. It wasn't like this was a blind date. I already knew Hunter.

"Hey," I greeted, hoping my nerves didn't show through my smile. "Long time no see." Damn, that sounded a lot less stupid in my head.

"Indeed." He returned my smile, giving me every indication he didn't notice or care how lame I was. "You look really nice, Mel."

"Really? Thanks!" I was just in shorts and a tank top, but they were the nicest thrift store buys I owned. "So do you."

He traded the T-shirt for a gray button down that

accentuated his tall, lean frame. The sleeves rolled up to his elbows showed off the slender, corded muscles of his forearms.

"I clean up nice when I got somewhere to be," he remarked with a lopsided grin and held his hand out. "Shall we?"

I nodded, and he took my outstretched fingers with a firm but gentle grip as I stepped out of the trailer.

"Have fun, kids. Don't do anything that I wouldn't do," Connor called after us.

"So, do everything! Got it," I shot back over my shoulder.

My boyfriend just laughed and closed the trailer door as I left for my carnival date with another man.

"Wow, he's really not bothered," Hunter mused as his fingers laced through mine. My heart collided against my ribs at the touch.

"Did you expect him to be?"

"No, I know he's a man of his word. I'm just more used to humans being so possessive of their mates. It's surprising when they don't treat their partners like property."

"I never thought about it like that," I mused as we walked through the carnival gate, waving to the ticket attendant who knew me as the ringmistress. No one recognized Hunter without his fur, teeth, and claws, and we preferred it that way.

"Hardly anyone does anymore, at least consciously." Hunter gave my hand an affectionate squeeze as we looked around at the attractions. The carnival had just opened for the day and some vendors and booth attendants were just setting up.

"Does it bother *you* being here?" I asked him. "Knowing what goes on behind the scenes?"

"In general, yes. I hate how exploitive this whole industry is, and not just of shifters. People like Connor, too." He smiled down at me. "But it's good to know this one isn't like that. And anyway, I'm here with you and determined to have a good time."

"Right. Sorry to talk about negative stuff."

"Don't be, Mel." His thumb stroked my palm. "So, what are you in the mood for? Food? Rides? Games?"

"Ooh, shaved ice!" I said, pointing. A cold dessert never sounded so good right then. At noon in the middle of summer in Mississippi, the humidity already hung in the air with a palpable thickness. Beads of sweat ran down the back of my neck like a lover's tongue and I prayed my makeup wouldn't start running.

Hunter stepped up to the truck with no hesitation and ordered for us. I got a pina colada flavored one, and he got a root beer float.

"Thanks." I accepted the frozen treat from him, swept up in the surreality of a guy buying something for me just because he wanted to.

"Thank the ringmistress. She got me a job," he winked, sticking a red plastic spoon in my cup of sugary ice.

A hula hooper danced for a small crowd not far away, so we sat down on a retaining wall to watch her and enjoy our shaved ice.

"What was your life like growing up?" I asked Hunter. "Did your pack have a lot of contact with humans?"

"We did at first," he answered, chopping at his own ice with the tiny spoon. "My pack was well known in a small town in Virginia, right on the edge of Jefferson National

Forest. My father was the town butcher and liked by everybody. My mother was a teacher at the local elementary school, where I attended with all the other human children. Back then it was in our best interest to integrate with human society as much as possible, while keeping our animal sides hidden."

I hesitated before pressing. "But that's not the case anymore?"

He spooned some shaved ice into his mouth and shook his head. "Some human locals saw my parents shift and started a witch hunt, or wolf hunt rather," he scoffed. "I was in high school at the time. Our alpha pulled all of us out for our own safety and we had minimal contact with humans since then. Whenever we did, we never stayed in one place long."

He set his cup down and rested both forearms on his knees. "It's hard because we're human, too. We want comforts like a bed, a shower, and a home with a roof. We want our children to be educated, have good careers, and stable families of their own. It sounds like an easy solution to just live as an animal for the rest of your life, but we crave human lives too."

"Shit, Hunter." I chewed my lip, the sweetness of the shaved ice now cloying on my tongue. "I'm sorry. This is supposed to be a fun day and I keep making you bring up heavy stuff."

"Don't worry about it." He nudged me with his elbow and shot me a heart-fluttering smile. "That's just life for a shifter. I don't mind talking about it. And anyway," he picked up my spoon, holding a big chunk of shaved ice near my mouth, "we're making new memories, better ones."

I parted my lips and allowed him to place the spoon on my tongue, watching him watch me with those sharp, golden eyes.

"And hopefully I'm giving Roo and Rinna a better life too," he concluded, breaking the intimate, brief spell between us to return his attention to the hula hooper.

"Are they okay alone while you're out here?" Hunter's children reminded me of my own siblings in many ways. Rambunctious, curious, and far too innocent for a world that could be so dark.

"Yes, they know not to leave the den when I'm away. It's instilled in all wolf pups when the adults go on long hunts. They're generally more independent than human children because of that."

"What do you think is best for shifters in general?" I asked, scraping the edges of my styrofoam cup. "Integrating with humans or staying far away from them?"

Hunter let out a long sigh and took a moment to answer. He looked like a marble statue as he thought—still, beautiful, and wise.

"If there was a way to be among humans peacefully, with the same rights and protections, and without being hunted for what we are, I think that would be best for everyone. Because it's impossible to hide from humans forever. Even if we created our own community away from everyone else, the wrong humans will undoubtedly try to round us up for their own gains. That's essentially what happened to my pack."

It made the most sense, but would be the most difficult to achieve. Just the public knowledge of shifter existence would throw the world into chaos.

I threw my now-empty cup in the nearby trash can and

wrapped my palm underneath his bicep. The slender muscle jumped at my contact.

"No more heavy conversations," I said in a mock stern voice. "Let's play some stupid games and try to win gigantic teddy bears and shit."

His face lit up immediately as he closed his opposite hand around mine.

"Shall we make it interesting?" he grinned wolfishly.

"How so?" I narrowed my eyes in suspicion as I stood from the wall, allowing my fingers to slide down his arm to his hand.

"The winner chooses what ride we go on afterward," he smirked, threading his fingers through mine as he followed. "Loser sucks it up and deals."

"Hah! Joke's on you. I love crazy rides," I declared. "Maybe I'll lose on purpose so you can give me all your spoils," I added with an exaggerated batting of my eyelashes.

"No way." He pointed at a balloon and darts booth up ahead. "That unicorn is mine."

"Yours or Rinna's?" I giggled. The plush unicorn on display was the size of a large dog, with a long golden horn and a rainbow-colored tail and mane.

"Mine," he repeated in mock seriousness before a smile cracked his face. "But will probably end up hers."

"Don't worry if you lose, I'll win it for you," I teased as we stepped up to the booth.

"Aren't you a little fox," he shot right back, his fingertips grazing my waist and lower back as he approached the attendant to pay.

It was the first time I heard anything resembling a

nickname from him, and the touching only made me hyper aware of that word's implications.

"I can't tell if that's a good or bad thing, coming from you."

He caught me in that golden gaze, as I'm sure many prey animals had been before. I felt captured, frozen to my spot, but not afraid.

"Good for you. Bad for me."

"Why's that?"

He handed cash to the booth attendant and accepted a handful of darts in return.

"Because a clever fox can drive a wolf crazy."

❧ 4 ❧

MELODY

Despite several tries, neither of us won the unicorn.

"I bet all of these games are rigged," I muttered as we walked away in defeat, both of our wallets much lighter without anything to show for it.

"Just 'cause they don't traffic shifters doesn't mean they're saints," Hunter chuckled.

We tried a few different game booths, losing badly at every one. The ring toss attendant felt bad enough that he gave us consolation prizes—toy squirt guns, which Hunter and I had too much fun chasing and shooting each other with.

After a few minutes of playfully squirting each other, I asked if we could call a truce. Hunter agreed. And then I stuck my gun under his shirt to blast his bare skin.

"Ah! This is what I'm talking about, you little fox," he growled playfully as I darted away, cackling.

He got me back just as badly—wrapping a long arm around my waist, holding my back against his chest while his other hand disappeared under the hem of my tank top. I barely had time to register how much of him was touching me when I felt the plastic nozzle against my bellybutton and the icy blast that followed.

"Ahhh! I give, I give! You win!" I shrieked.

"Not falling for that again." His warm breath fanned against my ear, his torso a solid wall of heat against my back. The contact of him against me almost distracted me from his relentless squirt gun assault until...

"Hunterrrr! It's dripping into my underwear!"

He released me, laughing so hard he nearly fell over.

"Say that louder. I don't think the whole carnival heard you," he gasped, before bursting into laughter again.

Meanwhile, I waddled around in a circle, bending over in front and trying to look behind to see if I appeared to pee myself.

"Maybe a few rides to dry ourselves off?" Hunter suggested, still chuckling as he wiped his eyes.

"Good idea, but I pick." I glared at him although I wasn't really mad. His eyes heated as I grabbed the wet spot on his shirt to pull him closer to me. "I dunno, though. I kind of like you in a wet shirt."

His arms slid around me and, despite their warmth, did nothing to soothe the goosebumps erected on my skin.

"I can say the same thing about you." His voice was laced with huskiness.

My forearms braced against his chest, but his heartbeat didn't feel nearly as fast or erratic as mine. One of his hands pressed a warm imprint between my shoulder blades, the other traced my jaw with the lightest brush of a fingertip. My gaze fell to his lips, where I saw a smile twitching to get out.

"What?" I asked.

"I was thinking," he said with a lip bite so small I almost missed it, "that I could make a joke about wet underwear, but I don't want to scare you away."

I couldn't help but laugh at that. "Really, Hunter? I got desensitized to offensive jokes when I was a toddler. You'd need to do a lot worse than that to scare me away."

He shrugged, bringing his caress on my face to a pause. "That's not really my style, anyway. Maybe Connor's influence."

I groaned, rolling my eyes skyward. He was absolutely right that Connor would not pass up the opportunity for an inappropriate joke. Neither would Razvan.

Stop. We are not thinking about him. Especially not right now.

"Well, whatever your style is, I want to learn about it." Feeling emboldened, I slid my hands up over his shoulders to wrap around his neck. "I want to learn all about *you*, Hunter."

His forehead lightly touched mine as his face grew closer. My pulse became a mad, rushing river in my ears as his lips filled my vision, parting as they nearly reached mine—

"OY! YOU, GIRL!"

I jumped back, startled at the voice that sounded like it yelled right next to my ear. Hunter immediately pulled me back tightly against him with a protective growl.

"Ya can do that cupcakin' later. We need to talk, girl."

The speaker was an ebony-skinned woman wearing a wraparound dress in a bright purple tribal pattern. Her hair was wrapped up in a matching purple fabric. She spoke with an accent I couldn't place and beckoned me with one long, purple fingernail.

A dark tent stood behind her with a wooden painted sign reading Madame Thembi - Fortune Teller.

"No thank you, ma'am," I smiled politely. "I'm not interested."

The woman's lips pulled back into a smile. "I'm not askin' ya, Melody."

Her jaws parted just enough to allow a long, slender, forked tongue to flick out and taste the air.

✭   *5*   ✭

MELODY

I blinked, and the serpent's tongue was gone. Only a bright, cheery smile with a slight gap in her front teeth shined on the woman's face.

"Ya know what I am. Don't act scared, girl." She nodded at Hunter. "Ya doggy boy can rip my throat out faster than I can strike. Ya have questions and if ya come in, I can find ya the answers."

"You don't have to, Mel," Hunter growled low next to my ear. "Just say the word and we can walk away."

"She's a shifter," I breathed, barely above a whisper.

"Yes, but something's off," he snarled. "She knows what I am, but she smells human to me."

That should have spurred me to move along and quickly. But I stood rooted to my spot, unable to take my eyes off the woman. She seemed thoroughly amused by my wide-eyed stare, chuckling and shaking her head.

"Do you know what I am?"

The words tumbled out as if someone else controlled

my mouth. I never voiced any of my questions to anyone, except when telling Connor about my dreams. He wrote them off as just that, dreams, but their vividness plagued my waking thoughts and sensations too. The more I tried to explain them away, the more vividly they came.

"Oh yes I do, girl," the woman's grin widened. "Never thought I'd see another one of ya in my lifetime, but here ya are."

Hearing that was enough to take one step toward her and then another.

"Mel!" Hunter hissed, pulling my arm back. "Are you sure?"

I looked back at him. "You and Razvan both said I smell human, but different. I've had... dreams and stuff involving you that I haven't told you because I don't know what any of it means." He said nothing as I wrapped my hands around his arm, just continued to eye the snake-shifter woman suspiciously. "Stay close to me just in case, but I really think she knows things about me that I don't."

His face hardened into a scowl, but he followed me to the woman's tent. She promptly flipped her fortune teller sign over to say CLOSED before pulling aside the black mesh curtain to let us in.

A spicy, smoky aroma filled my senses immediately. It wasn't bad, just incredibly strong. The dark tent was lit by dozens of small tea light candles, flickering with the slightest movement as we assembled inside.

Hunter immediately ducked to avoid hitting the various dried herbs, wind chimes, and talismans hanging from the ceiling. A low wooden coffee table sat in the middle of the tent with an assortment of crystals, incense, candles, and herbs strewn across its surface.

"Sit," the woman instructed, pointing to a pair of cushions across from the coffee table.

Hunter and I did so, his legs so long, he had to cross them at the ankles with his knees pointing straight up.

"Um, do I call you Madame Thembi?" I asked as the woman settled across the table from us.

"Thembi is fine," she said, blowing out the incense and waving her hand to dispel the smoke.

"How do you know what I am?" I asked, not caring to dance around the subject. "And what exactly is that?"

She let out a small, bubbly laugh. "Just like a shifter can sense another nearby shifter, a shaman can sense a shaman."

"A...what?"

"I couldn't sense you," Hunter growled. "But," he took a deep inhale, "you smell like Melody. Human with something else."

"Good boy!" Thembi praised with a small clap of her hands. "You're understanding now." If he'd been within reach, I'd have no doubt she would have patted his head.

Hunter's eyes narrowed and I could practically see his wolf form with bared teeth and ears pinned back.

"Fortunately for us," Thembi gestured between me and her, "we can sense shifters as well as our own kind."

"Our... own kind?" I repeated. "Are you saying I'm *not* human?"

"No, girl," Thembi huffed in annoyance. "Of course you're human. He told ya himself, ya smell like it. But," she leaned across the table, lowering her voice, "ya can give the illusion you're not." Her snake tongue flitted out again, proving her point and making me jump back off my seat.

"Not only that," she returned to sitting upright with a

laugh, "ya can sense when shifters are near. If one is in need, ya can feel him pull to ya. Ya know what I'm talkin' about, ah?"

I thought back to my first night working in Drowningville, when I only knew of Hunter as the fabled Wolf Man. In reality, he and his kids had been drugged and forced to partially shift in order to make them all look like werewolves—standing upright while covered in fur, not quite human or animal.

The ringmaster hyped it up for an entire week. Connor was convinced it was all a hoax, a scam to make people part with their money, but I still felt like I needed to see them. I couldn't understand why, but something in me pulled me to that stage like an invisible leash. And when most humans reacted with horror and fear, I saw him, caged and abused, and could only feel a heart-splitting sorrow.

And again with Razvan. Despite finding him too arrogant for his own good and intimidating as hell with all those tattoos covering him, I felt an inexplicable pull to him. When we walked together alone in the woods, and when he showed me his dragon form, I was never afraid for a moment. Honestly, I couldn't understand why other humans were so afraid of shifters.

"Yes," I breathed, returning my focus back to the smoky, dimly lit tent. "I felt them pull to me and I've had... interesting dreams."

"Ah-hah, I was just gettin' to that!" Thembi slapped her knees with another cheerful laugh. With each minute that passed, I felt myself relaxing. She was no threat, and I even began to like her. "What have ya seen, girl?"

I turned to Hunter, my heart threatening to leap out of

my throat. For some reason, I felt like I was about to confess a shameful secret.

"I saw you, in human form," I told him. "Before you approached me and Connor. That was how I knew you were the wolves we rescued. I recognized you from my dream." My eyes darted up to Thembi, hesitant to say the next part.

"Go on, girl," she encouraged, her whiskey-colored eyes sharp enough to see through my soul. "Tell the rest of it."

I swallowed and took a deep breath. "In most of my dreams, I feel like I *am* a shifter. I see through their eyes and experience what they're doing in animal form. And they feel so vivid, not like dreams at all but memories."

Hunter slid an arm around me, but I couldn't bring myself to meet his eyes. His lips pressed through my hair. At any point I would have been giddy, but he still didn't know. The worst was still to come.

"I think... I'm pretty sure," I choked to get the words out, "I saw through the eyes of your mate before she was killed."

In an instant, his body against me went from warm and comforting to stiff and cold. He pulled away to look at me with a harrowed expression.

"What makes you think that? How do you know it was her?"

"I was hunting with you," I explained. "I was a black wolf. You were the white one. We were stalking an elk herd."

His eyes doubled in size, and the color drained from his face.

"You were the distraction. I went in for the kill. That

was our strategy," I went on. "And I... Fuck, Hunter, I'm so sorry."

"You what?" Hunter demanded.

"I knew I was pregnant."

6

HUNTER

She didn't want to hurt me. The pained expression on her face told me that loud and clear, but it didn't stop the years-old wounds from reopening.

I saw the life leaving Audra's eyes just as clearly as I saw Mel in front of me. So much blood, and the final whispered plea she begged of me before I lost her.

"I'm so sorry, Hunter." Mel reached for me hesitantly, as if I would bite her. "I didn't know how to stop it. I didn't want to invade your privacy like that."

"I know." The words came out colder than intended, and she flinched. "When did you dream this?"

"Um." She composed herself to think. "Right before you talked to me and Connor that first time. So, almost two weeks ago?"

"How is that possible?" I directed the question at Thembi. "My mate died five years ago."

"Ah, nothin' ever truly dies, doggy boy," she waved an index finger at me. "Ya mate was taken in an abrupt and violent way. Her *yanna*, her spirit, is still earthbound. But ya cannot know or see that. Only a shaman can."

"So what, she's a ghost? And haunting Mel, or is Mel haunting her? And why the hell have *I* never heard of a shaman?"

The drudged-up memories and feelings I'd long since buried turned my mood sour and snappish. Mel and I had been having so much fun, too. I'd been fantasizing about kissing her for days, and it nearly happened. Now all I wanted to do was race through the woods on all fours. Alone.

"Down, boy." This woman really seemed to get a kick out of treating me like a dog. "Nah, she's no ghost. That term is too simple. And ya've never heard of a shaman because they're rare. It's a gift that is given, not inherited. Only another shaman can pass on the gift. Fewer and fewer have done so in recent years, so we are slowly dyin' out." She chuckled amusedly. "Like the dodo."

"So someone gave me these abilities?" Mel asked. "How is it given exactly?"

"Depends on the giver. You can direct your powers into an object and give that to someone. My master just did this." Thembi pressed her palm to her forehead. "Nothing happened, of course. I was a child and the gifts don't become apparent until ya turn eighteen."

"An object?" Mel suddenly slapped at her shorts and looked frantically through her pockets until she produced a coin that looked like a carnival token. "Like this?"

Thembi cackled delightedly as she slapped her knees. "It's startin' to make sense, ah, girl?"

"I still don't understand," Mel muttered. "Like, okay. Shamans have these powers and I've experienced these...

visions. But what's the point? *Why* am I seeing these things?"

"A good question." Thembi adjusted her seat. "The long-held belief is that shamans are the bridge between humans and shifters. They blend in with the humans but also protect shifters from inevitable conflict with humans. Centuries ago, shamans were far more numerous. Ya could find about ten shifters to one shaman. Shifters would flock toward shamans to be their human representative, more or less." She cleared her throat and shot us a knowing grin. "Because most shamans were female, she would find herself surrounded by multiple shifter men. I'm sure ya can see where I'm goin' with that."

An unmistakable blush rose in Mel's cheeks. If my dead ex-mate hadn't been brought to the forefront of my mind, I would have found it adorable. It made complete sense as to why Razvan and I were so drawn to her, and why she never showed an ounce of fear when we revealed ourselves.

"Why have shamans stopped passing on their gifts?" I asked. "It would seem like we need them now more than ever."

Thembi's jovial face turned into a frown. "Yes, shifters are in dire straits now, exactly because of the lack of shamans for them to turn to. With no humans on ya side, the rest are treatin' ya like livestock." She ran a hand down her face with a sigh. "Shamans used to be respected among humans, until public opinion started changin'. We started bein' seen as crazy people. Talkin' to animals and havin' visions didn't belong in a world with modern science and medicine. Nobody wanted to be targeted, so they stopped passin' on the gifts."

"That's a terrible reason," Mel echoed my thoughts. "Leaving shifters to suffer at the hands of humans with no one to back them up? Just because they didn't want to be made fun of?"

"It went beyond that, girl," Thembi replied in a scolding tone. "Some got locked up in institutions back in the day. Others even got hanged and drowned as witches, goin' way back. At the end of the day, people had to save their own hides."

"That's what it always comes down to," I muttered, more to myself than anyone else. "Survival."

Small fingers gave my palm a hesitant stroke. I closed my hand around Mel's, hoping she would see that I wasn't angry. I wouldn't lash out at her. I was just consumed by things I'd rather forget.

"Why can't I sense shifters or other shamans?" she asked, her voice sounding far away from me. "I didn't sense you just now."

"A gift still needs to be developed, girl," Thembi answered. "Ya need to practice listening. Stop all those chattering voices in ya head and listen to the deepest part of ya." She pointed at her own chest. "When did ya turn eighteen?"

"A few weeks ago," Mel replied.

"Hah! I'm surprised ya've had dreams already. That's half the battle, girl. Listen to ya instincts. Humans are animals too, don't forget."

Another set of fingers closed around my bicep, and Mel's voice became much closer.

"I think we need some time to process this. Will you still be here if I have more questions?"

"Yes, girl. 'Til the end of the carnival this weekend.

Take care of ya doggy boy. He's not a in good place right now."

A gentle pull to my feet and a few steps later, fresh air and sun hit my senses.

"Hey." Two hands flew to either side of my face and I found myself looking down into a pair of warm, brown eyes. "Are you okay?"

"Not really," I admitted. "You didn't mention it, so I don't think you saw what happened after the hunt."

Mel shook her head. "No, Hunter. I don't need to—"

"A hunter shot her," I said, my voice flat. "As she was dying, she begged me to take the pups and run. She was carrying two. Only one was alive." I looked toward the direction of the den, where the only two living memories of my mate remained. "That was Rinna."

"Oh, Hunter..."

Mel's arms went around my waist as she pressed her cheek to my chest.

"I'm so sorry," she murmured into my shirt. "I'll get a hang of this... gift, one way or another. I don't want to dig through your past. I don't want to bring up painful things for you or anyone."

"I know." I tucked her head under my chin and rubbed my hands across her back. "It doesn't hurt as much anymore, not like it used to. I just... didn't want to think about it again. Especially not today."

"Damn it." She looked up at me and huffed out a humorless laugh. "No matter what we do, we can't seem to have a fun, easy day, huh?"

I let out a heavy sigh, determined to get out from under the black cloud settling over me. "The day is still young, though." I stroked her face, trying to lose myself in those wide brown eyes instead of being haunted by cold dead ones.

"Let's go on some rides." I grabbed her hands and began walking us in the direction of the Ferris wheel and all the brightly lit rides surrounding it.

"You're seriously in the mood for rides?" Mel asked, catching up with my long strides.

"No, but I want to get out of this mood I'm in," I draped an arm over her shoulders, "and go back to enjoying my day with you."

7

MELODY

I had to admit, screaming my lungs out after a few hundred-foot drops felt incredibly cathartic. With Hunter grinning next to me, my feet dangling in midair, and the heavy ride harness secured over my chest, the day almost felt blissfully normal again. The adrenaline took over and I could forget about Thembi's haunting words for at least another few hours.

We were smart enough to get food *after* rides and walked through the vendor booths, checking out the clothes, jewelry, weapons, and other crafts as we munched on corn dogs. My stomach flipped uncomfortably as we strolled past the metalsmith tables. This was where I first saw Razvan, flipping knives flawlessly through the air like he was born to do it.

I half expected to see him here, maybe running his tattooed fingers over the array of sharp metal blades. Maybe with a girl or two on his arms as he showed off his skills for them, a preview before showing them what he could do with that split tongue.

I could still taste how that kiss felt, and thought about it more than I'd ever admit. He kissed me onstage in front of everyone on our opening night. The gentle caress on my lips from both sides of his tongue was unlike anything I ever felt before. And then it was over before I could blink. The crowd loved it, seeing it as part of his bad boy charm. But he cheated on his girlfriend by kissing me.

Maybe it was hypocritical of me, seeing as I was essentially dating Hunter *and* Connor, but I could never be with a man who kept other girls on the side. At least with my two guys, I felt like they valued me enough not to kiss anyone behind my back. And I wanted to make damn sure they knew I cared about them just as much.

The afternoon shadows grew long as we wrapped up our window shopping. Hunter kept his arm around me as we walked together, with the occasional squeeze of my shoulder or caress of my neck. I snuggled happily into his side with my arm around his waist. His long, lean muscles moved fluidly with each step and damn, he smelled good.

"What do you think, one last ride?" he suggested, looking up at the Ferris wheel.

I couldn't believe how late it had gotten already. The day flew by and I never wanted it to end.

"Okay," I said wistfully. "As long as it's a slow ride."

The moment we sat in the capsule and began the gentle ascent upward, Hunter wasted no time in getting cozy.

"No one can interrupt us now," he whispered against my hair, pulling me closer.

My heart crashing against my sternum, I turned to face him but found his eyes looking straight ahead.

Colorful lights, tents, and flags stood out against the

dense, dark forest. Organ music and joyful voices echoed through the grounds, floating up to us as gentle background noise. Hunter's eyes remained fixated on the dense trees in the distance, far away from people and lights.

"Don't blame yourself," I told him, placing a hand on his knee. "If you could have saved all of them, I'm sure you would have."

"I know," he sighed. "It's a decision I made peace with a long time ago, then buried it in the past. I had to move on for Roo and Rinna. Now it just feels like all that progress is undone."

"I'm so sorry!" I took one of his hands and squeezed it as if my newfound shaman powers could take away all his suffering. "I shouldn't have kept it from you, but I was so torn on telling you for exactly that reason."

"It's okay, Mel. Really. It sucks, but it has been a long time. It's nowhere near as painful as when losing her was fresh. All I can do is let the feeling pass."

The Ferris wheel paused as we reached the top. His arm around me felt snug and secure, holding me close to him like this date had no hiccups at all. Our temples leaned against each other as we quietly watched the carnival from our place in the sky. We were untouchable here. Despite everything trying to pull us back down, this quiet place, high and alone, gave us a sense of serenity.

"In a weird way," Hunter said softly. "I'm not *glad*, but I can appreciate everything that's happened. Losing her. Getting captured, all of it."

"How can you say that?" I turned to face him, my nose brushing his cheek.

He faced me, his mouth hovering within an inch of mine.

"Because it all led me to this moment with you."

I don't know who leaned in first. All I knew was our lips met—gently, but with intention. Our kiss unfolded like a slow, partnered dance. Hunter threaded his fingers through my hair with one hand, cupping my face sweetly with the other. He tasted warm, comforting, and oh-so-delicious. It felt like everything you'd imagine from kissing a romantic Disney prince.

But in his kiss, I also felt a hot undercurrent of raw masculinity and alpha confidence. Somehow I knew it was his wolf, the animal in him, feeling the urge to claim a mate, to dominate and possess. This confidence was quiet and primal, not brash and showing off. I felt it in the way he held the back of my neck as he explored my mouth further. I felt it in the way my whole body shivered when he ran a hand down my thigh.

"Ride's over. Two bucks if you want to stay on."

The bored attendant's voice barely registered in my mind. Hunter shifted in his seat to pull out some bills and tossed them to the attendant. His lips never fully separated from mine, not even when we smiled and giggled as we began another ride up.

I don't know how many times we went around, only that I couldn't get enough of Hunter's lips and tongue. Kissing him was so intoxicating, a light soreness tingled through my lips once we parted for a breath. I opened my eyes to find daylight quickly fading, giving way to a brilliant pink and purple sky.

"So much for just one ride," Hunter chuckled with a kiss to my cheek.

"How long have we been up here?" I giggled, curling my legs under me on the seat.

"No idea. I think I threw twenty bucks at him." His eyes flickered from my lips across my face, as if debating kissing me again. "I should probably get you back to Connor soon," he added.

"Connor is not my dad," I giggled, laying my head against his shoulder. "But you should probably get back to Roo and Rinna."

"Yeah," he sighed, sweeping the lightest of kisses across my mouth before standing and pulling me to my feet.

"Hey, um." I chewed my lip nervously as he led me off the platform and down the rusted metal steps, his fingers firmly laced through mine. "Do you want to do this again?"

"Are you kidding?"

His smile was electric as he lifted our connected hands and twirled me. I spun in place, feeling like a princess as I finished the twirl with my back pressed to his chest and his arm around my waist.

He kissed me tenderly, smiling against my lips. "I'd like nothing more." Somehow my jello legs didn't give out from underneath me as he unwrapped his arms and we resumed walking like normal people. "Maybe I'll take you dancing, though. I'm feeling a little sick of carnivals at this point."

I swung our hands back and forth between us as I gathered my nerves for the next question.

"Are you going to say anything to Roo and Rinna?"

"I'm not sure," he answered after a moment of thinking. "Maybe not in a super serious, obvious way. They know you and like you. They know *I* like you." He brought the back of my palm to his lips and placed a kiss there. "If this keeps going well, I think they'll figure it out naturally just from seeing us together."

"What if they ask questions?" I pulled his arm back over my shoulders.

"Then we answer them," he said lightly. "I don't lie to them about anything and you don't have to either." He stopped abruptly in his tracks and took a deep inhale. "There's a shifter nearby. Can you sense him?"

I looked around, only seeing a sea of carnival-goers.

"Not with your eyes. He's near, but is staying out of sight. Can you tell he's here?" He spoke low and close to my ear, giving the illusion of whispering sweet nothings to those passing by.

"No," I sighed in frustration. "I don't know how to sense them like you do."

"Remember what Thembi told you," he encouraged gently. "Quiet everything else and focus on your deeper instincts."

"How do I do that?"

"Close your eyes and tune everything out. Listen to the animal part of you. Not the human."

I felt stupid but did as he suggested anyway, taking a deep breath as I closed my eyes. Focusing on the weight of his arm on my shoulders like an anchor, all the voices and music of the carnival faded to a dull white noise.

The air seemed to shift direction as I tuned out the distractions. The smell of popcorn and deep-fried sugar faded away, replaced by... smoke?

A sense of comfort passed over me as I picked up the smoky smell, like I was in a cozy cabin with a roaring fireplace. A chill tried to nip at my skin, but the heat of the fire chased it away. This wasn't the swampy, humid forests of Mississippi anymore. This place felt much colder, cleaner. It also felt... unusual in a way I couldn't explain. Almost unreal and magical, like a place out of a fairytale.

Something hot and scaly brushed against my back, then a hard, sharp point like a knife dragged down my cheek. Both touches floated across me gently, like a caress. I didn't fear them, despite sensing the burning heat and power of this shifter. Whoever it was, they only wanted it to protect me. This person cared about me.

My eyes snapped open, the recognition hitting me like a brick wall.

"Razvan," I breathed. "It's Raz. He's here."

8

MELODY

Raz stepped out from behind a food cart, his inked skin and all black clothing giving him an ominous, dark presence over the bright, colorful carnival decor. He wore an apprehensive look on his face as he approached me and Hunter, like he might go back on this decision at any moment.

"Hey, Mel," he greeted dryly, hands shoved in his pockets casually, but the tension in his shoulders cut through the air like swords as he walked closer to us.

My heart clenched uncomfortably. I'd almost forgotten the smooth, dark honey of his voice, clipped with that lilting Romanian accent. The type of voice that every woman fantasized about whispering dirty things into her ears.

Still, I couldn't find my voice to answer. Thankfully, he focused on Hunter for a moment and stuck out a tattooed hand.

"I don't think we've formally met. I'm Razvan. Call me Raz."

"Evening, Raz. I'm Hunter." He accepted the dragon's handshake. "What are you up to tonight?"

Raz's steel-gray eyes flicked over to me. I clamped my mouth shut, biting the inside of my cheek. I said my piece to him already. There was nothing left to say and no reason for him to approach us.

"I didn't want to interrupt your time together," he shifted uncomfortably in his lace-up motorcycle boots. "But I was wondering if I could have a word with Mel for a few minutes."

"No." The word spat through my lips like a rotten piece of food. "I'm done talking to you."

"Mel... *steluța*." His voice strained with the plea as he stepped toward me. Hearing that name he used to call me was just another twist of the knife in my gut.

"Don't call me that," I hissed, stepping back and hiding halfway behind Hunter. The look of pain on Raz's face just about killed me too.

"Mel, please." Desperation laced his words. "This is a misunderstanding. Ally was never my girlfriend. She wanted that, but I never did. Not with her."

"So you used her," I spat from behind Hunter's arm. "She had feelings for you and you still slept with her. You lead her on. You *knew* kissing me would hurt her!"

"I..." He snapped his mouth shut and shook his head, scratching his nails through his dark hair buzzed close to his scalp. He couldn't even deny it, and that just made my heart hurt more.

"I'm not doing that anymore," he protested. "I don't want to hurt anyone, especially not you."

"I'm not hurt. I'm just fine." The lie tasted bitter on

my tongue. "I have Connor. And Hunter. I don't need a man who uses girls and discards them when he's bored."

"That's *not* what I am!"

He roared the denial with enough anger to make people stop and look at us. Mothers pulled their young children close as they hurried away. Thankfully, no one was close enough to catch the smoke wisping out of the corners of his mouth, nor the glow of fire just behind his teeth.

"Okay, this isn't getting us anywhere." Hunter stepped between us with a raised hand. "Both of you need to cool off if you want to have a productive conversation about this."

"I don't want to have *any* more conversations with him." My fingers dug into Hunter's forearm, though I couldn't seem to tear my gaze away from Raz.

"Razvan, dude," Hunter addressed him in a kind but firm tone. "If she doesn't want to talk to you, you need to respect that."

"You said you trusted me," he ignored Hunter, our gazes locked. "Why are you taking the word of some girl who almost attacked you over *me?*"

"I guess I was wrong to trust you," I answered as coldly as I could muster.

His handsome face morphed from shock to a frightening scowl of rage. Hunter pushed me further back behind him, his whole body rigid as he stared down at the furious dragon shifter.

"I'm not like all the men your trashy mother brought home, Melody," Razvan leaned forward as he spat the words, until his chest met Hunter's hand, braced out to keep a distance between us. "If you weren't such a damned stubborn child, you'd be able to see that."

"Back the hell up," Hunter growled, his teeth bared and looking longer than normal. "I'm warning you."

Raz blinked, jerking his eyes away from me and meeting Hunter's as if seeing him there for the first time. His twisted scowl remained. A low, rumbling canine growl escaped Hunter's chest. For a terrifying moment, I wondered if those two would actually get into it.

Raz broke eye contact first and stepped back with his hands raised.

"We're cool, wolf. I got no beef to hash out with you." Not even sparing me a glance, the tattooed dragon shifter turned and disappeared into the fading light.

Transfixed on watching the back of his black leather jacket become smaller as he walked off, I waited. I didn't dare take my eyes away, just in case.

But there was no hesitation, not even a glance over his shoulder as he walked away from me for probably the last time. When he was out of sight, I kept watching, my hope crumbling away with every passing second he didn't come back.

"Hey." Hunter tilted my chin up to face him, his golden eyes concerned and his teeth now human sized. "You okay?"

"Yeah, fine," I mumbled distractedly. A lie and he knew it.

He pulled me against him and rubbed a warm, soothing hand down my back. "He shouldn't have said that," he murmured with a kiss on my forehead. "It was uncalled for."

"It was true, though." I continued our walk out of the carnival grounds and back toward the campsite. "He was absolutely right."

"That doesn't mean he has to throw it in your face like that," Hunter replied with a soft growl. "He did that to hurt you and that's not cool, Mel."

Razvan was the one I opened up the most to about my past. I told him details I never even told Connor, like my alcoholic mom's endless string of boyfriends who were not only drunks themselves, but abusive to me and my siblings. And the fact that I didn't drink was because I learned alcoholism was often passed down from parent to child. I saw my older sister follow in my mother's footsteps and refused to let that be me.

Just knowing the potential to become that kind of person was inside me, unlocked by a certain substance, gave me massive self-worth issues growing up. I did okay in school, but no one wanted to be friends with me because I lived in the trailer park. Boys saw me as good enough to hook up with but never date, which prompted rumors about me being just like my mom—screwing every guy that looked her way and ending up pregnant too many times. And to no one's surprise, her baby daddies always bailed.

Razvan was sweet and a good listener when I opened up about not drinking, or at least he appeared to be. He then showed me his dragon shift and said I was the only human he had shown that form to. He certainly never indicated he would throw the shame of my upbringing in my face.

I *never* wanted to be like my mom and became overly

suspicious of men's motives as a result. And yet here I was, juggling my feelings for three guys at the same time. It was hard enough allowing myself to trust Connor and now Hunter. Because of them, I felt like I was finally allowed to breathe. I could relax, laugh, be myself, and fall in love.

My cantankerous soldier and the shape-shifting family man. For a fleeting moment, I thought Razvan could fit into our little band of misfits, too. But the moment his trust could be called into question, I was like a stretched out rubber band that snapped back. I regressed. I immediately went back to the mindset I knew all my life—that the only thing men cared about was getting their dicks wet.

And that was my fault. Not his.

"He did it because I hurt him first."

I didn't just see the hurt in his face. I felt it when I sensed him.

When his presence—or whatever it was I sensed—touched me, it did so with longing and sorrow. He missed me and it made me realize how much I missed him. I was right. It was wrong of him to kiss me with no warning and hurt Ally, but he was also right. I projected my own bullshit onto him, and that wasn't fair.

And I still pushed him away, lashed out at him, and for what? For no other reason than being a stubborn child, like he said.

Hunter and I walked in silence across the campgrounds to Connor's trailer, where a warm glow came from inside. My mood thoroughly soured, I hoped he wouldn't ask a million questions about this date. It seemed no matter how much Hunter and I just tried to have fun, something had to come along and ruin it for us.

"Hey, listen," the handsome wolf said softly, turning to face me in front of the door.

I peered up at him with reluctance as his arms slid around my waist and pulled me closer with a gentle tug.

"I don't care who or what tried to get in our way tonight," he lowered his forehead to mine, "I had an amazing time with you, and I can't wait to see you again."

"Hunter, it's okay. You don't have to say that," I murmured. "I'm a magnet for drama and bullshit. And I'm an immature teenager, I just make it worse—"

"Mel, stop."

He cupped one hand to my cheek and brought his lips crashing down to mine. The sudden pressure and intensity elicited a gasp from me, providing ample opportunity for his tongue to invade and deepen the kiss.

My knees wobbled under the weight of him, and his arms found their way to the small of my back, crushing me against his chest. If that kiss on the Ferris wheel was from a romantic fairy tale, this one was from a deep, dark fantasy. The charming prince had dropped his facade to reveal the hungry wolf underneath.

He left me breathless when he pulled away, and craving more than just a kiss. I clung to his shoulders, standing on tiptoe to reach his mouth again, but the kiss he returned was a soft echo of what just transpired.

He smiled against my lips, pulling away once more with reluctance. "If I don't stop now, I might not make it home to my kids."

"We wouldn't want that," I purred, pulling his head down to mine for just one more. Or maybe a few more.

Our date started to replay in my mind as I got my last few kisses in, and I remembered what he said about how shifters had human wants too. Secure homes, jobs, and schools. I suddenly felt incredibly shitty about this place with Connor, as small and junky as it was, while Hunter had to go back to the woods.

"Hey, tell me something honestly," I murmured, my hands drifting down to his chest.

"Anything," he said with a kiss to my forehead.

"Do you and the kids need a place to stay?" I looked up at him. "You know, somewhere nearby with a bed and a shower."

"We're fine, Mel. But thank you." I caught a hint of defensiveness in his voice, maybe with a bit of pride mixed in.

"Are you sure? Connor and I can pool together for a motel room or—"

"You've already done more than enough to help me." His gaze drifted across me, matching his fingertips that lightly traveled along my back. "I couldn't possibly ask you for more."

"It's no problem for us. Really," I insisted. "You and the kids deserve some basic comforts."

"And really, we're fine. I promise." His fingertips rubbed circles on my back. "We're basically camping now and they're enjoying it. When we get paid for closing night, I'll get us a trailer kind of like this one," he glanced up at Connor's RV, "probably a bit smaller, though."

I only remembered then that closing night—our final night of performing—was tomorrow. Then the carnival would close for the summer and we'd all be out of a job, left to return to a normal life or find another show to perform in.

"Where will you go after that?" I asked, fearing the answer.

He lifted one shoulder in a lazy shrug, running one affectionate finger from my jaw to my neck.

"I'll go anywhere I'm wanted."

❦ *9* ❦

MELODY

I didn't sleep a wink.

Connor snored softly next to me, having already passed out when Hunter and I finally parted for the night. The bottles of Vicodin and Jack Daniels next to the bed made my stomach drop when I walked in. He'd been trying to numb some kind of pain while I was away—whether in his legs, heart, or mind, I wouldn't find out until the next morning.

I held my lucky coin—my apparent source of power—above my head, alternating between turning it over between my fingers and closing my fist around it. How many times in my life had I looked at this thing, with its silver outer edge and gold inlay? With my newfound discovery, the crossed daggers stamped on both sides reminded me of grinning teeth.

A magician gave it to me at my first carnival, when I couldn't have been older than eight. He pulled it out from behind my ear, then placed it in my palm, closing my fingers around it with a white-gloved hand. As the only thing ever freely given to me, I treasured it ever since then.

In the darkness of Connor's trailer, I closed my fingers around it just as the magician did and held it to my chest. Closing my eyes, I searched hard for a clearer memory of the man who gave it to me. Did he say anything to me? Did I ever get a good look at his face?

And what confused me the most, why did he choose to pass on his shamanic gifts to *me?*

My memory of that moment was fuzzy at best. I had been distracted because of my mom stumbling around drunk and causing a scene. We may have gotten kicked out, but I wasn't sure.

I let out a sigh, released the coin from my fingers, and let it rest on my chest. It felt warm on my skin, most likely from me holding it so much. All my life, it had been the one object that held any value to me, the one thing that was mine and no one else's. It gave me comfort, strength, and confidence from dealing with my mom's drunken rages to strutting across a stage as ringmistress.

But it never felt *magical.* I certainly didn't notice anything different when I turned eighteen. I slept with it under my pillow the night before my birthday and slipped it in my pocket when I woke up before anyone else. Then, when I walked away from that so-called home for the last time, I ran my fingers across those stamped daggers and found the courage to never look back.

I remembered Thembi's forked tongue flicking between her teeth. What did she say? *"Of course you're human, girl! But ya can give the illusion that you're not."*

Okay, what is the point of that? I wondered. I had to talk to her again, hopefully before our show tomorrow, if I had time.

I held my hands up in front of my face, only their outline visible in the darkness. In my mind, I pictured them turning into paws with white fur and black nails, just like Hunter's. I stared at them until my arm muscles fatigued, then slapped them down to my sides with a heavy sigh.

How could I feel like anything *but* completely human when that was all I ever was?

I never truly felt the rush of a kill or the ground underneath my paws as Hunter did, nor fire in my lungs and the sensations of taking flight like Razvan. Only in my dreams.

My mind settled into the one I had last night, some sort of caged predator that felt completely different from a wolf. This animal was *huge* and felt powerful enough to kill a wolf with one swipe of its paw. But all it could do was pace back and forth, slowly going mad.

The humans walking by looked so smug, but I could smell their fear underneath. They had to keep me sedated round the clock just to feel safe enough, even after sticking me in this tiny cage. Gutless cowards with their tranquilizer guns and soft pink skin. One day they would pay, and they looked so damn delicious...

"Holy shit! What the—Mel?!"

Connor startled awake so quickly it jolted me out of the state I was in. He sat up in a flash and scooted across the bed away from me, as if afraid for his life.

"Babe, is that you?"

"Yeah." I blinked at him in the darkness. "You okay, Con?"

"I heard a noise, and I felt... something." He shook his

head, breathing deeply. "Must've been dreaming, but *fuck…*"

I scooted across the bed to him and leaned my head against his heart, which pounded like a drum against my cheek. His skin was hot, but a cold sweat covered him in moisture.

"What did you hear?" I kissed under his chin, curling my legs up and snuggling against him.

"It sounded like," he rubbed his forehead, "an animal growling. A bear or something huge like that. I swear it was so loud, like it was right on top of me. For a second, I thought I was going to be eaten alive." He let out a long exhale as his arms wrapped around me. "I had a bit of a rough evening, as you can see." He nodded toward the pain pills and whiskey.

I peered up at him. "Your legs? Or flashbacks?"

"Both," he mumbled ashamedly, looking away. "But I've never felt like an animal was about to maul me to death and eat me before." He forced a chuckle. "I think I'm finally losing it, babe."

"Stop." I cupped his cheek to make him look at me. "That wasn't you. I'm… pretty sure it was me."

Even in the darkness, I saw his forest green eyes narrow in confusion and gave him a quick rundown of our encounter with Thembi and my latest dream.

"A shaman?" he repeated. "You mean like the old Native American medicine man type of people?"

"I don't know, maybe?" I threw my hands up. "And these powers came to me on my eighteenth birthday, from a coin I've carried with me everywhere. I think *I'm* the one losing it, Con."

"You're definitely not losing it before me," he chuckled, with a kiss to my forehead. "It *kind of* makes sense." His fingers caressed up and down my arms as he pondered on it. "You can't shift, but you can channel the shifters, sorta. Like you were just thinking of this caged animal from your dream and suddenly I feel like I need to get the fuck away or I'm dead."

"That growl you heard," my fingers worked into the stiff knots in his shoulders, "I don't remember making it but I felt so angry and powerful, like I just wanted to kill something because it was what my instincts told me to do. I felt that just now in my *own* body."

"And I nearly pissed myself in fear while in bed with a gorgeous woman. *That's* never happened to me before."

He laughed when I smacked his chest in mock anger, but turned serious when he caught me staring at the pills and alcohol again.

"Please don't tell me you self-medicate like this often," I whispered, leaning my head on his shoulder.

"No, babe. I promise." He squeezed me tighter, pressing a kiss to my neck. "I just had an especially rough day today. It won't happen again."

"Any particular reason why?" I turned my head to rest my opposite cheek and found his lips hovering over my eyelids in the dark.

"Nothing important."

"Connor."

"Honestly, babe. It was stupid of me. I just... didn't want to deal with feeling shit from the past. But I swear to you," he cupped my nape and kissed me with so much passion it left me breathless, "I'm over it. I'm not doing that shit again."

My gaze fluttered away from his, still feeling uneasy. "If

you were feeling like that, I should have stayed with you. I shouldn't be out with another guy while you're struggling."

"Wrong," he said with a playful tap on my nose. "This is *precisely* why you should have someone like Hunter to spend time with. You shouldn't have to be burdened with my issues, babe. It's my shit to sort through, not yours."

"But I love you," I protested, nipping his lower lip. "And I want to be here for you when you're going through tough times. You shouldn't have to deal with that stuff alone."

"And I love you, babe. So much," he murmured, returning my kiss with a small, affectionate bite. "You help me in ways I can't even begin to explain. And you deserve better than to wade through the dark side of my mental illness. I'm not exaggerating. It's best that you don't see that side of me."

"You," I stabbed my index finger into his chest, "don't decide what I deserve, Connor. *I* do. And I'm going to prove to you I'm with you through thick and thin. Even if Hunter and I get together, I'm not gonna run to him every time you have a flashback. I'm staying by your side and helping you get through it because that's what love means to me."

I felt like a cup of water running over. The depths of what I felt for him rose to the surface and spilled over with no valve to shut it off. He opened his mouth to speak, and I raised a hand to cut him off, because there was no stopping this overflow.

"And I am *not*," I shuddered in a breath, "going to call 911 because someone I love overdosed on pain pills and alcohol *again*. I did that for my mom, my sister, even random men at our house because I was terrified they would die, and I'm *done*, Connor. I'm not letting it happen anymore."

He stared at me for a few moments, his expression unreadable, then said nothing as he shoved me away from him and scooted across the bed. Away from me.

I watched, hurt at first, then stunned, as he grabbed both the pills and the whiskey off the shelf. With both bottles in one hand, he slid open the window with the other and chucked both items outside. A second later, I heard the distinct sound of glass shattering.

"Never again," he said gruffly, returning to me and sliding his hands around my waist. "Because that's what love means to me."

I jumped into his arms at the same time he pulled me forward. Our lips and tongues crashed together in a frantic dance to seal the promises we just made. Holding me tight against his chest, he turned to lay me down on my back. His mouth never broke from mine as he hovered above me, settling his weight on his forearms, and then between my legs.

My moans silenced by his tongue, I yanked my tank top up over my breasts before wrapping my arms around his wide, muscular back to pull him down to me. It wasn't enough just to kiss him or even feel him inside me. I wanted his skin married to mine.

"Oh, babe," he groaned, kissing a hot trail down my neck as his heart beat against mine. He helped peel my top off my arms as my thighs wrapped around his hips and shimmied his boxers down his thighs.

His hips rolled against mine, bringing his cock to full

hardness as he teased my vulva with it. Every thrust of his shaft against my clit sent me gasping, digging my nails into his back as the ache inside me grew hungrier.

"Condoms," I murmured when he paused to kiss my nipples.

"Good girl. You remember."

"Shut up. Leave me alone."

He laughed, kissing me again as he reached above us to fumble on the shelf for the foil packets. After what felt like an agonizingly long wait, he pressed inside me and we both released a sigh of utmost bliss and contentment.

Connor wasn't my first sexual partner, but the first one I genuinely enjoyed it with. Even now, in this middle of the night quickie, every kiss and thrust felt like he was tailor made for my pleasure. His lips never left my skin. He murmured how much he loved me and how good I felt wrapped around him as he sank into me.

The moment my moans became whimpers, my breaths grew erratic, and the pressure began building in my core, he drew out my pleasure for as long as he could while delaying his own.

"Come with me," I pleaded in his ear. "I want to feel you."

"You first," he growled savagely at the restraint of holding himself back.

"I'm going to—oh, Connor!"

My orgasm lashed out like whips cracking along my nerves. At the same time, my pussy convulsed around him like it wouldn't let go. He shuddered and groaned, clenching his fist in my hair and grazing his teeth along my shoulder. Like coiled springs, we carried the tension to the point of no return, and then released.

But even as the tension left our bodies, we never let go of each other.

10

CONNOR

A burning hot pain pulled me out of sleep.

It concentrated around my stumps and for a moment, I was back on the black hawk minutes after being airlifted. The IED explosion itself never hurt—adrenaline and shock took care of that. It wasn't until I was laying on my back on a stretcher, looking up at the tear-streaked faces of my brothers in arms and then down at the bloody, mangled mess of my legs, that I felt the worst pain of my life.

I shouldn't have drank with the pain pills last night, least of all because it upset Mel, but they were taking too long to kick in and it was killing me. Now it all had worn off completely, and my dumbass threw them outside in the middle of the night.

Careful not to disturb Mel sleeping peacefully, I scooted to the end of the bed toward the door. My prosthetics leaned against the wall just in reach, but I looked away as if they were a bad omen. They were the reason my pain kept getting worse. After three years of wear, their custom fit had slid out of calibration. The more I wore them, the more pressure they put on the *wrong* areas of my stumps.

Fumbling on my boxer shorts, I winced as the fabric grazed over the smooth, rounded ends of where my legs stopped. It felt like knives dragging across my legs, like those masked thugs who laughed and threw rocks as I dragged my broken body across the desert—

Nope, don't go there. You're not there. You're here.

I turned to look at Mel, sleeping peacefully on her side. Her gorgeous curves made a long, sweeping line from her ankle to her shoulders. She was my anchor to reality. Thinking of her kept my head above water when the demons of my past tried to drown me. She reminded me I survived and my life now was worth holding onto.

Visibly, nothing was wrong with my legs, which only made me wonder if the pain was all in my head, too. No open wounds, no discoloration, nothing. But if it wasn't real, then the meds wouldn't have worked, right?

From the edge of the bed, I unlocked the door before lowering myself to the floor. Every brush of the floor on my legs made me want to howl in pain, so I lifted my hips up and used all the strength in my core to walk on my hands outside.

It was early enough for a chill to bite at the air, and no other performers seemed to be up yet. Even better.

I hand-walked alongside the trailer, my eyes sweeping for that orange prescription bottle. I spotted the shattered bottle of Jack right away and took care to not place my hands in broken glass.

"Fuckin' come on," I muttered, looking underneath the trailer and all around the tires. Nothing.

My mind raced as I thought about what I'd do for tonight, our closing show. I nearly passed out from the pain during my last act. I got out of my prosthetics as fast as I could and scored the Vicodin from one of Razvan's guys while Mel was busy. Yesterday's rest didn't help a lick.

I wouldn't make it through my act feeling like this. No chance in hell.

"Connor?"

Mel leaned out the trailer door, the bedsheet still wrapped around her and her big doe eyes hooded with sleep.

"Hey babe," I gritted my teeth through the burning, twisting, stabbing sensation as I rested my lower body on the ground.

"What are you doing?" She rubbed her eyes.

"Legs are killing me," I admitted. "I was looking for the pain pills I threw out here."

She rubbed her face, wide awake. "Oh, Con. Let me get dressed."

Fifteen minutes later, she had inspected every nook and cranny underneath and around the trailer. And we still turned up empty.

"Some junkie must've swiped it," I hissed, pulling myself up to the second step of the trailer so my legs could swing in midair.

"I have Midol." Mel squeezed my shoulder as she slipped past me back inside. "It's not as strong but might help."

I accepted the tablets and water from her, insisting on triple the normal dose despite her reluctance, then sat back and waited for the edge to come off, if at all. Like dark laser targets, her eyes never left me.

"How long has your pain been this bad?"

Fuck, I was in for it.

"Today makes three days."

"Three days?!" she repeated. "Why didn't you tell me yesterday?"

"Because you would have canceled your date with Hunter to be with my sorry ass."

"As I *should* have been!" She raked her fingers violently through her hair. "Connor, this is what I was talking about last night."

"What a coincidence," I huffed bitterly. "Same here."

"Con—"

"Did you have fun?"

She lifted her head from her hands. "What?"

"Did you have fun yesterday?" I asked. "With him, in spite of meeting a spooky fortune teller lady and wrapping your head around your shamanic powers."

"I... yes, I had fun. But Con—"

"Then it's a good thing you went," I told her. "Learning about yourself is just icing on top of that."

A heavy sigh escaped her as her shoulders sagged and her eyes closed. I realized I was testing her patience, but the sooner she figured this out, the better.

"Connor, there's no way you can perform like this. As ringmistress, I *do* have some sway and I will not put you through that."

"I'll be fine if this pain goes down at all. But I sure as hell am not sitting out, babe. We need the money too badly, cause who knows where we'll end up from here."

"And I need you to be *okay,* Connor." She took my hand, threading her small fingers through mine. "Can't we go to a doctor? What if it's—"

"No, babe," I said apologetically. "My benefits are completely tapped out. Even a routine visit will cost me thousands. I'll have to sell the RV if I get stuck with that, and then what? I'll be at rock bottom again and I can't do that to you."

"But it's not going to get better, is it?" Her dark eyes glittered with tears as they met mine. "You've been feeling like this for three days and it's not going away? That's serious, Connor. We need to see someone about it."

"After we get paid, maybe," I sighed. "But realistically, there's nothing we can do. We've got to pack up and drive to the next job, which is going to eat through whatever we make. Doctor's visits, new prosthetics, none of it's realistic for me. All I can do is keep kicking the can down the road."

Mel said nothing as her face hardened. Then she stood up abruptly and jumped the bottom step like she was heading out on a mission.

"Where are you going?"

"Where'd you get the Vicodin?" she asked. "If all we can do is numb your pain for now, that's what we'll do. So I'm getting you more."

I huffed out a dry laugh. "You're not gonna like the answer."

Her eyes narrowed. "Tell me."

"Razvan."

11

MELODY

Wandering through a campsite of scary, tattooed men was the last thing I wanted to do. Not to mention seeing Raz again so soon after our confrontation filled me with dread. But for Connor's pain relief, no price was too high.

Leers from Razvan's men, a group of fire breathers and knife throwers who called themselves the Flaming Swords, crawled across my skin like the legs of insects. The man sitting at the fire with the half-naked girl in his lap seemed too preoccupied to stare at me, so I chose him to approach.

"Excuse me," I said in as clear a voice as I could.

The girl looked up at me first, glaring daggers. The man slowly pulled his head away from her chest and regarded me with an annoyed expression.

"Can I help ye, ringmistress?"

His accent took me aback. I knew I'd seen him speaking Romanian with Raz and the others, but his lilt sounded Irish.

"I'm looking for Razvan."

"Aye." He threw an arm around the woman's shoulders and palmed her breast as if no one was watching. "And do ye see him?"

Of course, this guy was going to fuck with me. They would never make it easy on me.

"No." I offered a smile despite raging on the inside. "I'm wondering if you could tell me where he is?"

"In case ye haven't noticed," he replied with infuriating calm. "I've been a little busy with my pet here to keep track of his comings and goings. And trust me, ring-mistress," his eyes flicked up and down my body, "if he wanted to see ye, ye wouldn't need to ask me."

Before I could wrap my head around whether this guy was insulting me or not, a string of Romanian words flowed through air like music behind me. I turned to find a familiar pair of steel-gray eyes looking back at me.

"*Steluţa*," he murmured before catching himself and hardened his expression. "What are you doing here, Melody?"

Shit, shit, shit. I did *not* feel ready for this.

"Can I talk to you privately?" I could barely get the words out with my heart trying to force its way up my throat.

"I thought you were done talking to me."

His tone made me flinch, but I somehow forced myself to stand my ground, despite feeling like I would crumble at any moment.

"This isn't about me, or us." My nails dug into my palms. "It's Connor."

His eyebrows, lifting a fraction of an inch, were the

only sign of emotion on his face. He stared at me for so long I began to worry he'd tell me to go.

He abruptly turned to go back inside his tent. "Make it quick." He slapped the flap open and went inside, not bothering to hold it open for me.

Steeling myself, I followed him in and took a moment to let my eyes adjust.

The inside of the tent was open, roomy, and comfortable, like a rich hunter's pavilion. A worn Persian rug stretched out across the ground, its pattern faded from years of use but no less beautiful and intricate. At the far end of the pavilion, a king-sized air mattress laid on the floor. It was haphazardly covered in sheets and pillows, like the sleeper had been tossing and turning all night. Or having wild sex.

My stomach dropped at the thought of Razvan fucking Ally in that bed. Did they ever? Had he brought anyone else here? I shouldn't have cared, but the thoughts of him with anyone else bothered me immensely.

"So, what's up with Connor?" Razvan asked tersely. He folded his arms as he leaned against a table covered in an assortment of knives and swords. I couldn't help but notice all of them pointing straight at me.

"He's in a lot of pain," I answered, lifting my eyes from the polished steel to meet his. "I was hoping you could help him."

"My boys already gave him something for that," he growled. "Try again."

"It was my fault. I made him throw it away." My cheeks flamed. "He mixed it with alcohol and I kind of flipped out."

Raz gave me a long, calculated stare. "And what happened?"

"He threw the whole bottle out the window and it was gone the next morning."

He sighed deeply. A long stretch of silence passed between us and I could only begin to speculate about what he was thinking.

"So his pain has not gotten better?" he asked in a flat voice.

"No, it doesn't seem to be."

"Then he needs more than pain management."

I glanced up. "Believe me, I tried telling him that. But you know how stubborn he is."

Razvan huffed out a breath, regarding me cooly as he tipped his chin upward. He seemed to be deciding whether to stab, burn, or kiss me. If he chose the latter, I promised I wouldn't hold it against him this time.

"And why should I help again?" He ran his tongue along his teeth. "I was already generous once. Now I'm being begged again three days later? I'm reminded of a junkie that needs a fix."

"Connor is *not* a junkie!" I finally lost my cool.

"He mixed with booze, no?" Razvan rubbed the dark stubble on his jaw.

"He was having a really hard day. The pain is unbearable to him, Raz. He's really suffering." My desperation grew like a balloon on the verge of popping. At any moment, I was ready to fall to my knees and truly beg.

"Poor human," he sneered. "Yes, nothing but a life of pain and suffering. I wouldn't know anything about that, not even if I had to beg anyone for relief."

His sarcasm bled through like acid. Like Hunter, he'd

been sold to a carnival, abused and drugged for entertainment. But even worse, he was the first and only shifter in his family for generations. They had long since forgotten about their dragon heritage and saw his shift as a curse. His own family sold their son away.

I bit my tongue, fighting the urge to snap back. *You couldn't have suffered all that badly if you're still here.* But I truly didn't know why Razvan was still in this business now that he was free. And I couldn't make this about him and me again. I had to remember who I was here for.

"Raz, Connor's always been good to you. He considers you a friend. Can you please put aside whatever this is between you and me? For him? He'd do it for you."

"I'm not a pill dispensary," the tattooed dragon shifter growled. "I helped him once and was happy to do it. You fucked up and expect the same generosity again? Not happening, not without telling me what I get out of this."

"How about your full pay for closing night?" I crossed my arms, mimicking his stance. "Instead of getting cheated out of it?"

His eyes heated as his lips curled into a snarl. "What are you getting at?"

"Connor can't perform when he's in pain. If he's not part of the show, attendees will walk out. They might demand refunds. And they sure as hell won't see your act, or Hunter's, or anyone else's. His absence will make the whole show suffer, which means we all take the hit on our paychecks when this is over."

Another uncomfortable silence. He could take one of those knives on the table behind him and use it to cut the tension between us. The air in this tent felt stifling and hot. I couldn't begin to tell if it was the weather, his dragon shift heating up, or the mounting tension due to us being alone in this tent with its messy bed.

His shoulders cut through the air abruptly as he turned, rounding the table to rummage through a backpack leaning against one of the tent supports. I stood frozen, watching, not wanting to blow this chance by saying or doing something to make him change his mind.

After a moment, Raz returned to me, holding a small plastic baggie in his tattooed palm. Inside it were six white round tablets.

"This is not exactly the same, it's generic," he muttered. "But it'll do the job."

"Thank you, Razvan," I whispered, reaching toward his open palm.

Just before my skin could make contact with his, he closed his fingers around the pills and yanked it out of my reach.

"Remember, this has nothing to do with me and you," he snarled. "I'm covering my ass. And Connor owes me now."

I swallowed the dry lump in my throat. "Got it," I choked out. "I'll let him know."

Without another word, he dropped the baggie into my hand, seemingly careful to not touch my skin directly. It hurt more than I cared to admit.

"Was there anything else you needed?"

He posed the question coldly. Those gray eyes challenged me, daring me to answer a certain way.

I need you to be sorry for throwing my past in my face. I need to know you still want me and no one else. I need you to kiss me again and mean it.

"No," I answered just as coldly. "Nothing at all."

His expression twitched just slightly. For just a fleeting moment, I saw the raw, vulnerable side he revealed when he showed me his dragon shift. It passed over his face in a glimpse before the cold mask settled back over him.

"Then you may go."

He said it like another dare, but I wouldn't rise to his bait.

Clutching my prize in my fist, I turned my back on him and left.

12

CONNOR

"Are you sure?"

"Babe," I sighed. "My answer isn't gonna change, no matter how many times you ask me that. Yes, I feel fine."

Mel's brows furrowed extra hard as she applied her lipstick in the mirror.

"I'm just saying if you don't feel up to it, I can make something up in my announcements—"

"There's no need," I slipped a hand under her red tailcoat to wrap around the corset that defined her hourglass shape, "because I am just as fit as ever to perform." I moved her hair to drop a kiss to the back of her neck, enjoying the shiver that elicited through her.

"I just want you to be okay," she sighed in the mirror. "And I'm nervous, I guess. This is my last night as ringmistress. Who knows where we'll end up after tonight?"

"Doesn't matter," I murmured, pulling her back against me until my lips were in her hair. "I got you and you got me. And Hunter. And Razvan."

"Scratch that last one and you'd be right," she muttered, checking her makeup one last time before reaching for her top hat.

I looked at her in surprise. "You mean y'all didn't make up passionately when you went to get my pills?"

"No, quite the opposite in fact." She ran a hand along the brim of her top hat before twirling to face me. "We both made it very clear that it had nothing to do with us. We just want to see this show through, so we all get paid. And you owe him now, since he feels he was generous to you twice."

"Damn." I rubbed my jaw. "The two of you are being stubborn as fuck."

"You're one to talk," she jabbed with a playful smack to my chest.

"Takes one to know one." I slipped my mask in place and offered her my arm. "Ready, babe?"

"As ready as I'll ever be," she sighed, wrapping her hand around my bicep so we could walk backstage together.

I wished to reassure her, to tell her even bigger and better things awaited us after this was over. We'd be part of even grander shows and make enough money to not worry about anything. We'd develop our own following and people would travel across the country just to see us, no matter *where* we performed.

But we could just as likely find nothing. As much as I wanted to believe we'd come out on top, I didn't have it in me to make promises I couldn't keep. So I walked out proudly with my gorgeous ringmistress on my arm, taking in all the curious looks in our show attire. For all we knew, this would be our last night dressed up like this.

The backstage area buzzed with even more chaotic,

excited energy than the past few nights. Everyone could feel this was the ultimate night and prepared to give it their all.

"I'm going to check on Hunter," Mel said, giving me a quick air kiss to not mess up her lipstick.

"Sure you are," I teased, sitting down as I prepared to remove my normal prosthetics and put on my stilts.

Our wolf boy remained out of sight until he did his partial shift for the show. It was just safer for him if people didn't know what he looked like in human form.

She paused, giving me a worried glance as I popped off my legs. "Do you want me to stay?"

"No." I smacked her playfully with my longer leg. "Go on, girl. Get some of that doggy style love. I know you miss him."

"Connor," she groaned, rolling her eyes to the ceiling, but I didn't miss that smile twitching at her lips as she walked down the hall.

I enjoyed the view of her long legs walking away in those tights until she disappeared around the corner, then fitted on my stilts.

"You're on in ten, Connor," Nigel, the carnival manager, said in a clipped tone as he walked by in a hurry. He must've been especially busy, making sure closing night went off without a hitch.

Even so, that gave me plenty of time to walk around and warm up before showtime. I grabbed the curtain to pull myself up to my full stilted height of twelve feet. Running through my mental checklist, I took a few measured steps. Balance, weight distribution, pressure on my stumps, everything felt good.

I really do owe you, Raz, I thought. Maybe he would

consider the debt repaid if I talked him and Mel into making up. I loved that girl, but she wrote off a good guy before anything had a chance to blossom between them. Her instinct was to lash out defensively at the first sign of a guy being shady and with good reason. But this was the rare exception. She was wrong, and she just needed to admit that.

I hadn't seen much of Raz around either in the past week. He made good on his promise to give Mel some space, but when she hadn't come seeking him out, it sounded like things got ugly during her date with Hunter. She mentioned running into him before heading out to get my pills from him, but didn't want to talk about it further, which told me enough.

Shit. What was that?

A tingle shot up my leg, starting at my right stump, and traveled all the way to my groin. I'd been walking back and forth as I was thinking and felt completely normal up until now.

I took another few tentative steps and—*fuck!*

A zap of pain shot up my other leg. I grabbed one of the stage supports and hissed, grinding my teeth against the pain. I shifted my weight, trying to ease the pressure on my legs, which helped a little, but I couldn't do this for long. In a few minutes, I would be putting tremendous pressure on them.

Panic surged within me. Even if I had another pill, it would take too long to kick in.

The drums kicked up and all the lights onstage concentrated on a single spotlight. Shit, Mel was about to make announcements and then it'd be me. What the ever living *fuck* was I going to do?

My beautiful woman walked out from the opposite end of the stage, waving and smiling at the crowd who roared their greeting at her. Some of them had attended every single show. After being ringmistress for just a week, Mel was already developing a fan base. She just had a natural talent for captivating an audience. Somewhere underneath my pain-frazzled mind, I wondered if that was another expression of her shaman abilities.

"Ladies and gentlemen, boys and girls!" Her voice rang out through the speakers with warmth, confidence, and clarity. "As our final show for you tonight here at Crying Falls Summer Festival, it's a bittersweet feeling for all of us."

She paused to take in their boos and protests. No one wanted this to end.

"I know, I know." She brought a hand to her chest, commiserating with them. "So let's make this the most incredible, spectacular, unforgettable night, everyone! What do you say?"

The ensuing cheers and screams drowned out my groans and grunts as I released the stage support. Hundreds of tiny knives stabbed right where my legs fit snugly into the stilts and grew worse with every passing minute. Sweat dripped down my forehead, making my mask stick to my skin. But I had to bear it. I had to get through it. I wouldn't let Mel or anyone else down.

All I could do was call on my Marine training. The pain, discipline, thirst, and hunger that I lived through years ago strengthened me for this. I just had to get through the act that I could perform in my sleep, and then get out of these stilts as soon as possible.

"Our first act knows his way around the stage," Mel

winked as she began her suggestive introduction about me. "And trust me, ladies, those long wooden legs aren't compensating for anything else!"

The onstage drummer hit a *ba-dum-tss* on his drum set, and even I laughed along with the crowd.

"Ladies and gentlemen, please give it up for Stilts, the entrancing acrobatic stilt walker!"

Just stepping onto the stage made me bite my cheek against the pain. Thankfully, no one could see my face behind the mask, but I had no way to keep from screaming while they were silent.

My music started up, and I got into my routine, which unfortunately started with variations of balancing on one leg. Nothing looked different as far as I could tell, but a few jumps of one leg to the other had me seeing black dots in the corner of my vision. Fuck, this was not good. I didn't feel this bad the previous night until the end.

I switched it up, diving my torso to the floor to press myself into a handstand. Mel would notice the change in routine but hopefully not figure out why. The crowd oohed and gasped as I walked on my hands across the stage. My legs felt slightly better without the pressure of the floor, but I couldn't do this forever. Not if we were going to give them a show worthy of closing night.

I dropped my legs behind me to come back up to standing, then immediately jumped into a backflip and *god fucking damn it, holy shit!*

It hurt so badly I almost missed the landing. The crowd didn't notice me cover my stumble and burst into applause while I took a small bow to recompose myself.

That had to be the worst pain in my life. It took all my strength just to stay poised for the performance when all I wanted to do was curl into a ball and scream. And the climax of my act involved multiple backflips going across the entire stage. Right then, just reaching the end of my act felt like an insurmountable obstacle.

Bear down and do your job. You are a Marine. Just get through it.

I ground my teeth so hard against the stabbing fire in my legs, I expected to not have any left in my jaws if I lived through this. Taking a few deep breaths, I leaned into the hell, wracking my body and did a few more tricks across the stage. I couldn't think or hear anything through my brain screaming at me to stop this.

Every step felt like my legs being cut off all over again, but I pushed through. The audience had to notice me struggling at this point. I couldn't complete my act and pretend like everything was totally fine. My body could barely handle one or the other, but not both.

Time escaped me. I had no idea if seconds or minutes passed when I reached my breaking point. My vision began clouding, and I felt cold all over, despite being covered in sweat. But I had to do my finale. I had to. I couldn't let my girl down.

I stuck one leg out in front of me, preparing to throw it over my head for my final series of backflips. Throwing what little strength I had into my standing leg, I pushed off. That fraction-of-a-second moment of levitating in the air felt so peaceful. My pain briefly disappeared before the darkness swallowed me.

13

MELODY

I knew right away something was terribly wrong.

Connor changed up his routine right at the beginning and seemed more off-balance and uncoordinated than usual. My nails cut into my palms as I watched him, wishing I could read his face.

"Nigel," I grabbed the arm of the carnival manager as he tried to walk by, obviously very busy, "something's wrong with Connor."

He paused, turning to look at the stage from behind the curtain with me.

"Damn right. He's wobbling like a baby giraffe." He looked at me expectantly. "Something you want to tell me, Mel?"

I swallowed, debating frantically in my head if I should tell him. Connor would be furious. He had too much damn pride and never wanted to let anyone know he was hurting, including me. But he and Nigel had a close professional relationship. They were both ex-military and Nigel was one of the few good people in the carnival business. If anyone should know besides me, it would have to be him.

"He's been dealing with really severe pain in his legs for a few days," I admitted. "Medication has helped, but it doesn't go away when it wears off. He took some an hour ago but... it doesn't look like it's working now."

Nigel's eyes fixated on Connor, who looked moments away from toppling over.

"What the hell are you doing, boy?" he muttered to himself.

The crowd gasped as he narrowly landed a shaky somersault and vaulted a few steps to maintain his balance.

"Shit. He's going to fucking kill himself." Nigel placed a hand on my arm. "You keep watching him. I'm calling an ambulance."

The weight of those words didn't hit me until he had already gone. Panic squeezed around my heart as my eyes locked onto Connor, looking more dazed and unsteady with each passing second.

"Come on, babe. Just stop," I pleaded. "Fuck the show, just *please* stop putting yourself through this."

I grabbed the curtain to physically stop myself from running out onto the stage. He seemed determined to see this through to the end.

"Oh no," I whispered. He was preparing for a backflip.

From the moment he kicked his leg out, I knew he wouldn't make the landing. My heart stopped. He was in the air, and then he was falling.

A scream rang out so loud it hurt my ears. My legs acted on their own, but it still felt like swimming through mud to reach him. I couldn't go fast enough. Only an eternity later, when I kneeled over his lifeless body laying on the stage, did I realize the screaming came from me.

"Connor! Connor!"

I yelled his name over and over as if that would wake him up. Chaos swirled around in my peripheral vision, but my focus remained on him. I didn't touch him. Somewhere in the back of my mind, a memory surfaced of a CPR class I took. Never touch someone who hit their head. It could make a neck injury worse.

Oh God, Connor! Life was unfair enough to him with taking his legs away. If he became paralyzed or brain dead, God or whoever had a sick sense of humor.

Someone grabbed my shoulders and pulled me away from him, then a bunch of people in dark blue uniforms swarmed in like ants to surround him.

"No! Get away!" I screamed, pushing and fighting against whoever touched me. "Don't move him, he hit his head!"

"Mel, shh!" Strong arms crushed me to a chest covered in tattoos. "They're the EMTs. They'll take care of him, *steluţa*." Hands stroked my hair in an effort to be soothing. This person smelled like leather, cloves, and smoke.

My brain couldn't even register who this person was. I just struggled to get a glimpse of Connor as they lifted him onto a stretcher. So many voices, so many people. But he was the only one that mattered. I couldn't lose him, not yet.

"Where are they taking him?" I demanded, struggling against the tattooed arms that held me. The team of EMTs began carrying Connor off the stage. Nigel was saying something into a microphone I couldn't understand.

"To the hospital," a deep, velvety voice rumbled against my ear. "They said we can follow."

"I need to go," I protested, pushing against the warm, broad chest to no avail. "I need to be with him."

A flash of pale hair caught my eye, and only then did my composure break. Or the shock wore off, I wasn't sure.

"HUNTER!" I cried through a rattled sob.

His golden eyes fixated on me, filled with worry and concern. Whoever held me finally let go, and I ran to my tall, beautiful wolf.

"What happened?" he asked as I crashed into him, ugly-crying into his chest. "I heard screaming and a bunch of commotion up here."

"Connor fell," someone spoke with an accent from behind me. "He hit his head and is being rushed to the emergency room."

I turned to see Razvan standing there, arms crossed, with a grim expression on his face. My mind reeled. Was he the one who pulled me away from Connor?

"We can follow them, though?" Hunter rubbed my back. His heartbeat against my cheek was the only thing keeping me from losing it.

"Yes, that's what they said." Razvan paused. "I take it you don't have a vehicle?"

"No, but I can follow the scent and run over there. I need to tell my pups where I'll be."

"Bring them. I'm sure they'll want to see Connor too when he wakes up."

Snippets of conversations drifted in and out of my awareness, but all I could do was hold onto Hunter and think back to right before the show started.

I shouldn't have left him. I should have stayed. Maybe

I could have talked him out of going onstage. God fucking damnit, I knew what he was dealing with and still left him to go make out with Hunter. How selfish could I be?

"Hey, little fox." A thumb stroked my cheek and my head tilted up to gaze at Hunter's handsome, angular face. "Raz has a truck. Would you be okay riding with him to the hospital and I'll meet you there?"

"I need you." I clung to his shirt. "Please don't leave me."

"I'm not, Mel. I promise." He lowered his forehead to mine. "I need to tell the kids, then we're all coming to keep you company. You're not alone, Mel. You never will be, not anymore."

Maybe it was his tone or the fact that I could feel him speak from pressing against his chest, but his words got through to me. Everything filtered out of my frantic, worried mind, but his words cemented in there like anchors. They kept me grounded and holding onto what little control I still grasped.

A calmness came over me, and I nodded, meeting his eyes to show that I understood.

His lips curved into a small smile as he kissed me, brief but full of sweetness and comfort. "Go with Razvan," he told me gently as he stepped away. "I'll be right there. I promise."

"Okay," I whispered, watching his back jog away before turning to Raz.

He merely jerked his head to the side and proceeded to walk in that direction. "Follow me."

I did as he instructed, moving my legs robotically across the stage. Thanks to Hunter's calming presence, my surroundings began to filter in as my panic subsided.

Everyone was leaving. The crowd moved in a single massive swarm toward the exits. Holy shit, there were so many people! I couldn't catch anything but murmurs, but they had to be disappointed. Maybe Nigel announced the show being canceled? Some audience members stayed where they were, watching us curiously as if we'd go back on like nothing happened. Not a snowball's chance in hell.

Razvan walked quickly off the stage and through the carnival grounds to his campsite. I hurried to catch up, trying not to teeter over in my heels. He never slowed enough for me to walk beside him, and maybe that was intentional. Less awkward that way. Neither of us would feel forced to talk.

"Give me a minute," he muttered when we reached his campsite. "I have to unhitch my trailer from the truck."

"Okay." I stayed by the fire, which had burned down to embers at this point.

He unhitched the truck in what had to be under a minute. I wondered if his dragon strength had anything to do with it.

"Let's go." He opened the passenger door and walked around the front to hop into the driver's seat.

I climbed in without hesitation, but stayed glued to the far side of the cab, away from him. Buckling my seatbelt, I closed the door, but left it unlocked and leaned against it. This kept me far away from Raz and would get me out faster when we arrived.

If he noticed or cared that I sat clear across the cab from him, he didn't mention it. He turned the key, and the truck roared to life.

"How far is the hospital?" I asked as we left the campsite and turned onto the main road.

"Not far," he answered. "Ten, maybe fifteen minutes."

Silence stretched on between us. I didn't get the sense that he felt angry or cold toward me, but all this empty space between us still felt wrong. I glanced at him, his face neutral and focused on the road as if he was driving alone.

"Did the EMTs say anything else?" My words felt weak. I could hear my own desperation to fill the silence with any kind of connection from him.

"Just where they were taking him, and that he was alive but unconscious," he replied flatly.

I turned to look out the window. Trees whizzed by, the space between them growing as we began to leave the forest and return to civilization. I looked for flashes of white fur, like when Connor and I first came out here. Seeing Hunter's wolf in the corner of my vision freaked me out back then. I thought I was going crazy, but now I was looking for a source of comfort. A reminder that everything was going to be okay.

"They should have worked."

Razvan spoke abruptly, startling me as I turned to look back at him.

"What?"

"The pills I gave him. They shouldn't have worn off so quickly." His jaw tense, he spat the words out through gritted teeth. I just then noticed his knuckles were white as he gripped the steering wheel. "I swear on my life, Mel. I'd never try to hurt him or sabotage his act. You and he are the only humans who know what I am."

"Raz," I breathed, unbuckling my seatbelt without thinking and sliding across the seat to sit next to him. "It's okay. I know you'd never do that."

He glanced at me once before returning his eyes to the

road. "You believe me?" he asked in a pained voice. "They're going to question me, you know."

"I do believe you." I placed a hand on his arm, soaking up the heat from his inked skin. "I trust you, Raz. I--," my voice choked with emotion. So many deep emotions swirling through me for three very different men.

"I've always trusted you," I whispered, lowering my eyes. "I'm just an idiot. You were right. I'm so sorry, Raz."

He took one hand off the steering wheel and wrapped it around mine, his tattooed thumb rubbing gently across my palm.

"I am too. I'm sorry, *steluţa*."

14

MELODY

e both jumped out of the truck the moment Razvan pulled into a parking space at the hospital. He grabbed my hand immediately and pulled me close as we walked up. I leaned into him, grateful for his presence now that this obstacle had moved between us. Perhaps it wasn't completely out of the way, but it had definitely moved.

Nigel was already in the lobby, standing at the counter when we arrived.

"Where is he?" I demanded when we burst through the doors.

He turned, glanced quickly at my hand entwined with Raz's, then lifted his eyes back up to me.

"They're running tests on him. X-rays and all that. I'm just finding out where our waiting room is."

After a few minutes, a nurse gave him directions and the three of us started for the elevator. Razvan pulled me tight against his chest and kissed my forehead when the door slid closed. His heart beat erratically underneath my ear and I couldn't tell which of us was more worried.

I slid my hands up his back, enjoying the momentary distraction of feeling his warmth and the contours of his body. He wasn't as tall as Hunter, nor as muscle-bound as Connor, but a perfect balance of strength and leanness. The decorations of ink covering him only highlighted the artistic lines and shapes his body made.

Choosing not to comment on our affection, Nigel looked away politely as the elevator ascended to Connor's floor.

The elevator dinged and the door couldn't slide open fast enough as we piled out. Nigel approached the desk and told them who we came to see.

The receptionist typed at the computer for a few moments and then glanced up at me.

"Are you Victoria Miller?"

"Um, no." I narrowed my eyes, puzzled.

"Okay, well, she's listed as a domestic partner on his emergency contact form. You all are welcome to wait and we'll give updates, but if there are any life-altering decisions regarding Mr. Shaw, we can only discuss those matters with her."

"Wait," I protested. "I'm pretty sure that's his ex fiancee. They're not together anymore."

"We have to go off of what's on his current emergency contact form, ma'am. If he's lucid enough to update it later, we will surely do that. In the meantime, y'all can have a seat."

Raz gently turned me away from the desk and led me to the waiting area. He sat me down, keeping an arm around me the whole time. Nigel sat across from us and immediately picked up a magazine.

I felt beyond useless just sitting there waiting, but Raz's fingers were soothing on my arms. That gentle touch, an anchor to keep me grounded, to keep me from standing up and bursting through the door to find wherever Connor was.

Some time later, the elevator dinged as it opened and the two children running up to me couldn't help but bring a smile to my face.

"Miss Mel, don't be sad," Rinna looked up at me with her gigantic blue eyes and crawled into my lap when I opened my arms. "Mr. Connor is strong, he's okay."

"Thanks, sweetie." I hugged her close. "I know, it's just hard not to worry."

Roo placed a small hand on my knees, his brow furrowed and golden eyes sharp. "Connor will be alright," he said in an adorably serious voice. "I know he will."

My aching heart eased just a little at how sweet these two were being. "Thanks, Roo," I whispered, fighting back tears.

"Any news?" Hunter picked up Roo and set him in his lap as he sat on the other side of me. His eyes flickered to Raz's arm around me, but his face remained cool.

"They're running tests. No updates yet."

Hunter nodded and placed a hand on my knee, gently circling his fingers in a massage. The simple gesture almost made me burst out sobbing. With Raz to lean on one way, Hunter on the other, and his two kids with their bright, adorable innocence, I never felt so supported before in my life.

Even Nigel, pointedly ignoring our affection with his

nose in a magazine, was at least here for me and Connor. He seemed almost like a dad figure, from what little I knew about that.

So this was how it felt to have people there for you. A support network always sounded like such an alien concept to me. "Lean on your friends when you need them. Tell your parents when you're having a difficult time. They want the best for you." I had those ideas drummed into my head at school while growing up, and they were always so laughable. I never had anyone.

And now, since abandoning everything I knew and joining this freak show, I had people here for me. And I swore to God I would never let this go.

I threaded my fingers through Hunter's, kissed Rinna on top of her head, then leaned my head against Razvan's shoulder. I wasn't alone anymore, and neither was Connor.

The wait was long and would've felt even longer if I had no one. The guys took turns getting up and grabbing snacks from vending machines. Roo and Rinna played with some toys and picture books in the waiting room. No one said much. My eyes stayed glued to the door. I didn't want to get up for a single second.

When it finally opened, I jumped out of my seat. A tall, slender man with glasses and a white coat turned to us with a smile.

"Hi, I'm Dr. Harman. Are y'all here for Connor Shaw?"

"Yes," I answered quickly. "How is he?"

"Are you Victoria?"

I sighed, hoping this wouldn't become an issue in letting me see him. "No, I'm Melody. His girlfriend. He and Victoria are no longer together."

"I see." His eyes swept over me, still in my ringmistress

outfit, then glanced to Razvan and Hunter. "Well, you can come on back so we can chat. Just bear in mind that the rooms are small."

"Go ahead, Mel. We'll wait here." Hunter gave me an encouraging smile. "Bring back good news for us."

I nodded, swallowing the lump in my throat as I followed the doctor through the door to a small exam room.

"First off, Connor is stable and not under any life-threatening conditions," the doctor began. He smiled at my massive sigh of relief. "He did sustain a concussion from his fall though, so we're keeping him sedated for the night and monitoring his brain activity."

"Thank you," I breathed.

The doctor opened a folder and flipped through some pages.

"Were you with Connor at the time of the accident?"

"Um, nearby," I answered. "He fell while doing an act onstage, you see," I gestured to my outfit. "I was backstage, watching. And I was with him right before."

Dr. Harman leaned against the hospital bed, making the sheet of paper over it crinkle. "If you don't mind, I'd like to ask you some questions, miss Melody."

I froze. "What kind of questions?"

"Questions that will help us give him the best treatment for when he leaves here." He pulled a ballpoint pen from his coat pocket and clicked the top. "I promise you, anything you tell me will be confidential."

"Okay," I said hesitantly.

He hovered the pen over the papers in the folder. "Is Connor currently on any medications?"

"Um," I chewed my lip. "He was taking some for pain."

"What was he taking?"

"Vicodin, at first. Then something else, I'm not sure."

"Did he have a prescription for this medication?"

I chewed my lip. "Um, no."

He paused and looked up at me. "Where did he get it from?"

"I don't know," I answered firmly.

The doctor scribbled some notes but didn't press any further. "Do you know what kind of pain he was having?"

"In his legs," I answered. "He also, um…"

"It's okay, Melody," the doctor said in a soothing voice. "We're trying to help Connor as best we can. It's vitally important for his recovery that you tell me everything you can."

"He has PTSD," I admitted, looking down at my feet. "He's been having flashbacks."

"I see, thank you for telling me." He jotted down more notes. "To your knowledge, has he received any treatment or therapy for his PTSD?"

"I'm not sure."

"To your knowledge, does he have a history of substance abuse? Alcohol, pain medication, other illicit drugs?"

"No."

The questions continued for another several minutes. My shoulders sagged with relief when the doctor closed the folder and returned the pen to his pocket.

"We're going to keep Connor overnight to monitor his brain from the concussion. When he wakes up tomorrow, I'll also work with him to find the source of pain in his legs and see what we can do for that."

"Can I see him?" I asked eagerly.

"Of course," he smiled. "He's asleep, but you can visit him briefly."

He led me to another room with a hospital bed propped up and an unconscious man lying in it. I barely recognized Connor, and it took everything in me to not burst into tears.

They shaved his head and placed those sticky monitoring nodes in several places. An IV was placed in his arm. Machines near him beeped and whirred. One of them showed what seemed to be a scan of his brain.

But he looked absolutely peaceful, eyes closed and breathing with deep, even breaths, as if he was sleeping right next to me.

"He's not in any pain right now," the doctor assured me. "I'll authorize a morphine drip for tomorrow when he wakes up."

"Thank you again." I looked up at him with heartfelt gratitude.

He nodded curtly. "I'll give you two a moment alone."

Except for the beeping machines and Connor's breathing, silence filled the room when he left.

"Hey babe," I whispered, approaching the hospital bed. "You're gonna lose your shit when you wake up in here."

A giggle escaped me as I took his hand. I was exhausted and still worried, but that didn't make the mental image of Connor flipping out at being in the hospital any less funny.

"I don't care if we get stuck with some huge hospital bill," I told his sleeping form. "No price is too high to have you come back to me." My hand drifted up to his handsome face and stroked his cheek. "But you've *got* to take your ex fiancee off your emergency contact form."

15

RAZVAN

Mel came out and updated us on Connor's condition a half hour later. She wanted to spend the night at the hospital, but Hunter and I convinced her to come back to the carnival campgrounds.

"You need to sleep, *steluța*," I told her. "And shower and change clothes."

"But I..." Her lower lip wobbled, and she sucked in a breath. My heart ached for her, but my dragon flared with jealousy. She cared about him so much. I had to remind the beast inside me that she had every reason to.

"I don't want to be alone," she admitted.

"You won't be." I pulled her into my arms. "We'll get your things from Connor's and then you're staying with me."

She stiffened a little, but I sensed it was more out of surprise than anything else. Then I felt her head nod against my chest. Good. I made a point of telling her and not asking.

"I'm staying with you, too!" Hunter's young son, a spitting image of the tall pale wolf, wrapped his arm around Mel's leg and hugged tightly. His daughter soon followed suit on Mel's other leg.

"Guys." Hunter kneeled beside his children to speak to them. "We're going home for the night and then tomorrow—"

"No, it's fine, Hunter," I told him. "You're all welcome to stay. I have a tent they can use."

He looked up at me, eyes sharp. "Are you sure? I don't want to impose."

"You're not imposing. Mel needs us right now. All of us."

His lip curled into the barest hint of a snarl as he stared me down. We couldn't work it out here in a human hospital, but I knew what he was doing. I returned his gaze, my own stare unflinching. Although we were completely different species, his wolf and my dragon understood each other.

Bringing his children into my territory, a foreign place without him sniffing out first, was a risk. He was letting me know what he would do if I ever compromised their safety. And I let him know that while they would be just as safe as Mel, it was *my* territory and I was the alpha there, no matter who else came in.

Hunter put his teeth away and lowered his eyes, accepting my offer and my position over him while we were there. It would be the exact opposite if I were to stay in his space.

With that settled, we all dragged our feet out of the hospital.

"The carnival is getting torn down tomorrow," Nigel

told us when we reached the parking lot. "But I'll work it out with the county that y'all can stay until Connor is fit to be discharged. I know someone who'll give me wiggle room on the permits."

"Thank you, Nigel, for everything," Mel released me and went to hug our manager. He reeled back, startled, then awkwardly patted her back.

"Ah, come here you old slave driver." I pulled him into another unwanted hug as soon as Mel released him. Although he worked behind the scenes, Nigel was a hero to improving work conditions for carnival performers. Unbeknownst to him, he was an ally to shifters as well.

He literally pulled me out of a wooden crate at one of the most vile carnivals in the country. As far as he knew, he was rescuing exploited immigrant workers. He even taught me English. Little did he know how much more he was doing. At least five other shifters had been with me, but all were too proud to accept help from a human. They went their separate ways, and I often wondered if they remained free like I was. Especially Arjun, that damn tiger shifter. A powerful beast but too strong willed for his own good.

"I'll count up your paychecks tonight," Nigel said when he finally wrangled himself away from me. A grim look crossed over his face. "I'll give y'all as much as I can, but I gotta be honest. The closing show going down like this isn't gonna be good."

"I'm fine with that," Mel said quickly. "We'll figure it out."

We said our goodbyes, then Mel and I piled into my truck. This time, she didn't hesitate at all about sitting close to me. I kept my arm around her shoulder as I steered the truck back through the winding forest roads with one hand.

"Penny for your thoughts?" I quipped after we drove several minutes in dead silence.

"I feel guilty," she said after a moment of pondering. "Like I betrayed him."

"Why?"

"He wanted nothing to do with hospitals. I'm certain he didn't want me telling anyone about his PTSD or his leg pain, either. They're going to treat him, which is great, but he was right. Someone's got to pay for it and we might end up homeless because of this."

"Homeless is better than dead," I answered. "You did the right thing and so did Nigel."

"He's going to be so pissed at me, though," she sighed. "I mean, I'm glad he'll be alive to be pissed, but I just know it's going to be a fight. He'd rather be some kind of martyr than seek every possible treatment available."

"I'll back you up," I promised, stroking my thumb on her arm. "So will Hunter. He's allowed to be pissed about whatever, but we won't let him take it out on you. You did this because you love him. If he can't see that for what it is, he's a fucking idiot."

"Thank you, Raz," she whispered, snuggling into my shoulder.

I dropped a kiss on her forehead as we drove on in comfortable silence, but something gnawed at me. Was I shooting myself in the foot here? I was being an emotional support for her right now, which I was happy to do, but what about when Connor got better? Would she still need me like this? Or would she go back to hating my existence?

We pulled up to Connor's trailer, and I waited in the

truck while she showered and changed her clothes. Then it was a short drive back to my campsite, where we could finally wind down and relax.

Most of my men were already breaking down tents and packing up belongings. We only gathered as a group for Nigel's carnival. Unlike me, they were humans with lives and jobs outside of the carnival world. I gave them a quick rundown of what was happening and wished them well. By morning, only my stuff would still be here.

"I didn't think I'd have company over," I said sheepishly as I led Mel into my main tent, quickly putting away my collection of knives and tidying the place up. She stood in the middle of my antique rug, a Persian relic I stole, looking uncomfortable and kept glancing at my bed.

"Raz?" she asked in a small voice.

"Yes, *steluța?*" I approached her, fighting the urge to pull her into my arms again.

"Have you been with anyone else?" her eyes flickered from me to the bed nervously. "Since Ally?"

I almost laughed. My little star was just as jealous as my dragon.

"No," I answered, taking hold of her hands. "I've been... waiting for you to feel ready to talk to me." A grin escaped me. "Without yelling or throwing insults."

"I'm sorry, Raz." Her eyes glittered with tears. "You were right. I was just being stupid and stubborn. I didn't want to admit I was wrong."

"I'm sorry, too." She pressed her face to my chest, and I stroked her hair. "You were also right. I led her on and that was wrong of me, whether she was a crazy bitch or not. I don't want to be a man that..." I exhaled deeply. "That breaks hearts."

Her head lifted slowly as she peered up at me, and I wiped the tears that just began to escape her gorgeous dark eyes.

"Do you regret kissing me?"

My hand trailed down her cheek to cup the side of her face.

"Do you want the truth?"

"Always."

"Not for a second," I answered, my breath hitching. "Maybe the circumstances, yes. But I'll never regret kissing you if it's the last one I taste."

Her chin tilted up, lips parted. I lowered my forehead until it grazed against hers. Our noses touched, and I just felt her soft breath fan against my mouth before my own mouth opened.

"Miss Melody! Mister Razvan!"

A child yelled for us right outside our tent just as our lips touched and we jerked away from each other, already breathless and panting.

"Hey Roo," Mel laughed nervously at the boy, who poked his head into the tent. "You found us."

"Dad, I found them!" he announced proudly.

I stepped out to find Hunter just outside, holding his daughter with an amused expression on his face.

"Roo, boy. You need to knock before poking your head into tents," he chuckled, ruffling his son's hair when the boy reattached himself to his father's leg.

"There was no door. How could I knock?"

"Scratch at the flap."

I cleared my throat. "Right, I'll get a tent set up for you and the little ones."

Turning to the fire pit, I huffed out a quick breath to ignite the logs into a warm blaze again before walking off.

"Whoa! Did you see that!" Roo exclaimed.

Mel, Hunter, and his family talked in low voices by the fire while I got the smaller tent up in a few minutes. By the time I finished, a mouthwatering smell wafted in from their direction and I realized I was starving.

"I brought food," Hunter said when I rejoined the group. "It's the least I could for you offering your hospitality."

I muttered my thanks and took a seat on a tree stump next to Mel, who was already tearing into a drumstick.

"You know, some vegetables wouldn't kill you guys," she teased, wiping her mouth. "Or a little mashed potatoes with gravy..."

"Human stomachs," I joked with a jab to her ribs before helping myself to a whole, small game bird roasting over the fire. "So picky. Hunter and I are carnivores. Our tastes are simple."

All of us were apparently famished. Not long after the food disappeared, Hunter's kids began nodding off, their eyelids fluttering.

"I guess that's goodnight for us," the wolf gently patted his kids awake. "See you in the morn—"

"Hunter, wait."

He looked at Mel, surprised.

She chewed her lip for a moment without speaking. "Stay with me tonight?" She darted a glance at me, then back to him. "With us?"

Hunter's gaze moved to me, then lowered just a centimeter. Fire bloomed in my chest. Yes, the wolf knew his place. In my territory, he had to ask me for permission. But the truth of the matter was, Mel could ask for anything and I'd give it to her without a second thought. If she wanted a wolf and a dragon to keep her company all night, that was no question.

I nodded sharply, and he returned it.

"Let me get them to sleep first," he whispered, then walked to the tent with his pups in tow.

Mel immediately turned to me and, before I could open my mouth, stammered, "I just don't want to be alone tonight. I'm not in the mood for... you know. I'm sorry, I just can't stop thinking about him."

"Shush, *steluţa*. It's okay." I pulled her into a hug, feeling her shudder with relief against my chest. "You have nothing to apologize for. Besides," I pulled away just enough to look at her. "We've just gotten back into each other's good graces. We don't need to fuck each other's brains out yet."

She dropped her head back to my chest, pressing her cheek to my heart. "I just figured that was what you expected."

The words stung, but I tried not to take them personally. My reputation preceded me and Mel was still hard-wired to think that all men wanted just one thing at any cost. But with patience and time, I was changing, and so was she.

"Even if I did," I murmured against her hair. "You can always tell me no. Always and I'll listen. You understand?"

She nodded, but looked unsure. "And if I do... you won't go to anyone else?"

"Absolutely not." I cupped her chin. "I'm not going to screw things up with the only human woman who not only knows the truth about me, but accepts me for what I am."

My thumb brushed against her lower lip. "As long as you want me around, my fire is yours."

Finally, her gorgeous face relaxed into a genuine smile that made my hard, scaly heart flutter. "You really do know how to be romantic. I'm impressed, Raz."

"I'm working on it," I chuckled, leading her by the hand back to the tent. "But I'm warning you now, I'm no Romeo."

"More like Dracula," she laughed, squeezing my palm. "I think I like that better."

Be still, my heart.

Hunter joined us a few minutes later, after Mel and I already changed into sleeping clothes and cuddled underneath the blankets on my king-sized air mattress.

"I'm not interrupting anything, am I?" he asked, amusement in his voice as his pale form approached us.

"No, but you're missing out on a good snuggle." Mel patted the space in front of her. "Get in. There's plenty of room."

Hunter paused by the bed, then swiftly removed his shirt and jeans, stripping down to his boxers. I felt Mel's breath hitch and her heat rate speed up as she watched him undress and climb into bed. I suppressed a grin as his arm wrapped around her waist, accidentally brushing mine on her hip.

"Sorry, Raz," he muttered.

"It's quite alright, wolf," I laughed, my breath fanning across the back of Mel's neck.. "I don't give a fuck if I touch you or not. As long as our girl feels safe and comfortable."

"Thank you, guys," she whispered, clasping her hand over mine and kissing Hunter from the sound of it. "For being here. For taking me to the hospital, just... every-thing. I don't know what I'd do without either of you."

"We're happy to do it, little fox." More kissing sounds and I swallowed the jealousy burning in me.

I settled with dropping a kiss to her shoulder, longing to taste her lips again, but I would be patient. She found Hunter and Connor worthy of that, but not me. Not yet.

"We just want you to be okay, *steluța*," I murmured behind her ear. "And we care about Connor, too. We're here for both of you."

She shifted between Hunter and me, turning around to face me. Without a word, her hands felt for me in the dark, finding my face. Her fingertips brushed against my lips and I kissed them before they slid around to my neck.

Then her mouth found mine, kissing me hesitantly at first, but then deeply. I fell asleep with a smile on my face and the sweet taste of her on my tongue.

16

MELODY

A tattooed arm around my waist. A pale, sculpted chest beneath my ear.

I slept so deeply, I almost forgot about last night. Looking at both of them, Hunter and Razvan both looked so peaceful, yet completely different in the morning light filtering through. And how lucky was I? Sandwiched between two gorgeous men. All I needed was my third.

Connor! He would be awake today! The thought startled me into action. I carefully lifted Raz's arm off of me and crawled over Hunter's long torso to reach my clothes on the floor. Raz groaned and rolled over, stopping inches away from Hunter. One more half-roll and those two would be cuddling.

I suppressed a giggle as I looked at them. If I had just walked in, there'd be no doubt in my mind those two were lovers. The thought sent a rush of heat to my core so fast, it made me gasp. My nipples hardened into tense peaks with no stimulation, despite it already being a hot and muggy morning.

I never thought much of two men being together, but the mental image of those two could not be erased. Down here in the south, it was definitely frowned upon, but I heard about places like California where it was celebrated more openly. I rubbed my face and went back to getting dressed, but the thought could not be unthought. And my body could not stop responding to it like it was the hottest thing since dragon fire.

I hardly dared to wake them up, but I was dying to know how Connor was doing. And I didn't want Roo and Rinna asking questions I didn't want to answer.

"Hunter," I whispered, tip-toeing to his side of the bed.

He looked like a marble statue. His platinum hair spilled across the pillows, his face turned to the side, showing off his statuesque profile as he breathed deeply. And his body. I half expected his pale skin to feel like the cold touch of stone as I gently shook his shoulder. But he was oh so real, living and breathing.

"Mmph." He turned his head and shifted, his hand clasping around mine as his eyelids cracked open lazily. "Hi, beautiful," he croaked, his voice groggy with sleep.

My heart skipped a beat. How on earth did I get so lucky? "Hi, handsome wolf," I returned.

Both of his arms reached for me. "Why're you wearing so much clothing? Come back to bed." He glanced at Razvan inches away. "I think someone else wants the middle, though."

Giggling, I pulled on his hands to bring him upright. "You should check on the kids. I want to go see Connor as soon as we can."

"Alright," he sighed, swinging his legs down to the floor. His snug boxer briefs left little to the imagination, though I'd already seen him naked.

Razvan muttered something in his sleep and rolled over again, settling on his stomach as he hugged Hunter's pillow.

"Have fun waking him." Hunter kissed my cheek after pulling on yesterday's jeans and shirt. "I'll be back when the rugrats are up."

With the blankets thrown back and the soft morning light filling the tent, I took a moment to admire the art covering Razvan's back. A single, massive tattoo of a dragon, twisting and winding through smoke and fire, covered his entire back from his neck and disappearing under the band of his boxers. From the black scales inked on the backs of his thighs, the tattoo seemed to continue over his entire backside.

The dragon seemed to inflate with smoke with every inhale and release bright burning flame with every one of Raz's exhales. It looked so alive and vivid, like it moved not just with his breaths but on its own.

Before I knew it, my hands were tracing the beast's scales, following its movement like it was a real creature that wrapped around me protectively. My hands felt warm human skin beneath them, but my mind felt armored scales that almost burned to the touch.

I closed my eyes and quieted my human mind as I was learning to do, tapping into the power that was bestowed upon me. Smoke floated around me, fire burned in my lungs, reptilian vision and instincts matched with intelligence and cunning beyond what human minds were capable. So this was what being a dragon felt like.

"Mm, Mel?"

The sensations faded as I opened my eyes. Razvan had flipped onto his back and blinked up at me.

"Good morning," I chirped awkwardly.

His gray eyes narrowed. "I swore I felt another dragon beside me, then I looked up and it was you."

"Yeah," I breathed, raking my hands through my tangled hair. "Hunter and I had an eventful date even before you crashed it."

I filled him in on what I told Connor about Thembi, quickly thinking I needed to keep these three guys together as much as possible. It was tiring repeating myself.

"A shaman, huh?" He turned on his side and propped himself up on one elbow, scratching his jaw with the other hand. "One of the shifters I'd been caged with years ago talked about shamans."

He said it so casually, but I still winced at the mention of him and others being exploited like that.

"What did he say?"

"A lot similar to what you just said. Poor cat held out hope that one would find us and rescue us. He said they looked human, but we'd just know when one of them came along." He smiled at me. "I knew you were different, *steluța,* but it was so long ago that I never put two and two together."

"I can't stop wondering why he gave it to *me,*" I sighed. "I was a child, barely bigger than a toddler. And my drunk ass mom got us all kicked out of there."

"Maybe it's not entirely gifted," he suggested. "Maybe there's something in you that was always there. He saw it and knew you were the right one to pass this torch to."

"I still feel so clueless about it," I admitted. "I want to use it to help more shifters, but I have no idea what I'm doing. And then there's Connor—"

"Sshh." He sat up, wrapping me in a warm embrace that instantly soothed like the comforting heat of a campfire. "One thing at a time," he murmured, rocking me gently. "Connor first, and then all the enslaved shifters in the world."

"No pressure or anything," I snorted.

He loosened his hold and looked at me with wide, metallic eyes.

"You've already done the unheard of by saving Hunter and me. So many shifters have lost hope that anyone is on their side. Word will travel fast, *steluţa*. And just knowing you're out there and that you care will light a fire under so many asses."

"That's sweet." I touched his face. "But I didn't save you. You were already free."

He smiled, his thumb caressing across my cheek.

"You did, *steluţa*. In ways you can't imagine."

THE FIVE OF us pulled up to the hospital a half-hour later. Roo and Rinna had never ridden in a car before, so I sidled up next to Raz. Roo sat next to me, and Hunter sat at the far end with Rinna in his lap. Raz indulged Roo by driving over every bump and pothole in the road, making the boy scream and laugh in delight with every jump and jolt through the truck cab.

"You don't have to fuck up your tires just to keep them entertained, Raz."

Rinna immediately clapped a hand over her father's mouth and narrowed her eyes in a stern expression. "Don't say bad words, Daddy."

"Sorry, sweetie. I forget sometimes." He smacked a big kiss on her cheek and I thought my heart couldn't melt anymore.

"It's alright, Hunter," Raz returned, smirking as his eyes remained glued to the road. "I got a good warranty on these. If I pop one, I'll get a brand new one for free."

We were all in high spirits as we pulled up to the hospital. I drummed my fingers with nervous excitement in the elevator, determined to stay positive and not assume the worst.

I launched out of the elevator as soon as we reached the floor, gripping the edge of the reception desk like a lifeline.

"Hi, we're here to see Connor Shaw," I said in a single, rushed breath.

A different receptionist from yesterday typed on the computer for a few moments before shooting me a friendly smile.

"You can go right in. He's awake and already receiving visitors."

"Oh," I said, surprised. It had to be Nigel. "Thanks!" I returned her smile and walked around to the side door as fast as my legs could carry me.

Remembering where the doctor escorted me last time, I rushed past nurses and other hospital staff in my eagerness to see my grumpy Marine boyfriend. And then my feet abruptly froze when I looked through the window of his room.

He was awake alright, and talking to someone. A

woman with a short blond bob sitting at the edge of his bed.

No, it couldn't be...

My feet wanted to run in the other direction, but I forced them forward as I turned the knob on his door. I had to know.

"...doll face."

Connor stopped talking abruptly, and they both looked at me as I crossed the threshold.

"Mel," Connor said, sitting up straighter. "Hey."

Mel. Not *babe*. While I swore, he just called *her* doll face.

I looked at the woman now facing me, with red painted lips and an adorable button nose. Her cropped blonde hair framed her face in sensual waves. Not just a doll face, but a goddamn Marilyn Monroe clone.

"Who are you?" I demanded, not bothering to mince words.

Connor cleared his throat. "Mel, this is Vicky. She was my, ah..."

"Fiancee," she finished for him.

CONNOR

My head felt stuffed with cotton, but the pain was gone. I groaned and started to move my fingers and toes. Wait, I didn't have toes.

Gingerly, I moved my head from side to side. No neck injury. The only concrete thought I could form through the fog that wrapped around me and even seemed to go through me. I cracked my eyes open to a room that was entirely too bright.

"Good morning, Mr. Shaw," a male voice greeted me.

"Where am I?" I groaned.

"You're at Crying Falls emergency hospital, Connor. I'm Doctor Harman. You had a pretty serious fall."

Hospital? Fuck.

"I can't be here." Pressing my hands into whatever surface I laid on, I began scooting my hips away. "I can't afford a hospital. This'll ruin everything. I can't do that to Mel."

"Calm down, Connor." Two hands grabbed my arms to still me. "Please calm down. We'll work out payment later.

But you've had a concussion and you don't have any prosthetic legs with you."

Damn it. Fucking hell.

I relented, not wanting to fight against a guy doing his job and especially when I wouldn't get very far. I sat back, blinking to make my eyes adjust to this stupidly bright-ass room. Details began to filter in despite my head still feeling fogged up. This was a hospital, alright. A skinny guy in his early forties, wearing glasses and a white coat, stood next to my bedside.

"I promise I'll discharge you as soon as I can," he said, dragging over a stool to sit on. "In the meantime, how are you feeling, Connor?"

"Foggy as fuck," I grumbled. "But the pain's gone."

"You suffered a pretty serious concussion," he explained. "Fortunately, your scans didn't show any skull fractures or bleeding in the brain. However, your brain *is* injured and you may encounter headaches, dizziness, or sensitivity to light for the next several weeks."

"Fantastic," I murmured.

He took off his glasses and wiped them on his coat. "The young lady with you said you were in pain as well?"

Thanks, babe. Always looking out for me.

I sighed. If I couldn't get out of here, I might as well reap the benefits of having to stay. "Yes, in my stumps."

"Would you mind describing it for me and how long you've been feeling it?"

I told him every detail I could recall in my fog-addled brain. He applied pressure to my legs and even tapped them with that reflex thing they used to make your leg kick out when you were a kid.

"I'm not a specialist when it comes to amputations,

Connor," the doctor mused as he finished. "But my best guess is you have some pinched or pressured nerves around your amputation points. You wear prosthetics, yes?"

"Yeah," I grunted.

"When did you last have them calibrated? They're most likely putting pressure on your nerves in a way that's triggering a pain response."

"When I got them," I muttered. "Three years ago."

The doctor's eyes widened behind his glasses. "You really need to recalibrate them, Connor. Otherwise the pain will continue and you'll prefer spending time in a wheelchair."

"Not gonna happen," I snarled. "Either of those options. I can't afford to get them recalibrated. Why do you think I'm a goddamn carnival performer? And I'd rather deal with the pain than spend my life in a wheelchair."

The doctor sighed and pressed his lips tightly together. "I'll make some calls to a few specialists I know. You're a veteran, correct?" he nodded at the dog tags around my neck. "There should be some way we can help you."

"Trust me, I hear that all the time," I answered. "And then that's the last I hear of it. I've exhausted all options, doc. You know as well as I do that I'm just one of thousands of vets this country has fucked over."

His mouth pressed even smaller, seeming determined. "I'll make those calls, anyway. You know never know what we might find." He stood to leave and quickly turned back to me. "Are you feeling up for visitors? A whole gang of people came to see you yesterday."

"Sure," I muttered, although I wasn't really feeling up

to seeing anyone but Mel. Not that I wanted her to see me like this, but those big doe eyes might make me feel a little better.

"I'll let the front desk know. Just hit the call button if you need anything."

Just as he left, I spotted a TV remote next to my bed. Sure enough, one click turned on the small screen up in the corner of the room. I settled back against my pillows and found a college football game to watch. Damn, how long had it been since I did this? Kicking back and watching a football game was a simple pleasure I once took for granted.

I was so into the game I didn't notice the blonde woman outside my room until she pushed my door open.

"Connor?"

My eyes met hers, and my heart stopped. My whole body went rigid. Her hair changed, but her face was exactly the same.

"Vicky," I barked, probably harsher than necessary from the way she flinched. "What are you doing here?"

"The hospital called me," she said, hovering by the door. "I guess I'm still your emergency contact."

I leaned back on my pillows, looking up toward the ceiling. "I guess I forgot about changing that."

"Connor, what happened?" she allowed the door to close behind her and took a few tentative steps toward my bed.

"Not important," I shot back. "You shouldn't be here. They never should have called you."

"Connor, I drove all the way up from Florida to be here," she argued, coming closer still. "Believe it or not, I was worried about you. I at least deserve an explanation."

My teeth grated against each other in my jaws. I forgot how annoying it was when she ignored my requests to be alone. At first, when we were still together, I thought it was just my PTSD. In hindsight, it was just a glaring sign of our incompatibility.

Not like with Mel. My babe could get through to me even when I pushed her away at first. She understood me even when we butted heads. I wanted her here, not this woman who now felt like a stranger to me.

"I got nothing for you, Vicky," I answered, throwing my hands up. "I'm not some decorated war hero like you wanted me to be. I'm the same curmudgeonly old bastard, probably days away from being homeless again. I don't know what you expected when you came up here, but sorry to say I'm just as disappointing now as when you left me."

"I've been texting you," she said, as if everything I just told her went right over her head. "Why did you stop answering?"

"Because I'm busy. And," I paused and leaned forward, unable to help myself from rubbing it in her face, "I'm seeing someone."

Her crimson painted mouth made a little 'o' of surprise. "You are?"

"Yeah, and apparently so are you." The rock on her left ring finger nearly blinded me.

She grabbed the engagement ring with her other hand and twisted it around her finger. "It's complicated," she muttered. "I'm actually having second thoughts."

"Well, good luck with your life and whatever," I sighed, my patience growing thinner by the minute. "But it's got nothing to do with me now. And I don't care to pretend to be buddies or whatever the fuck so you can delete my number."

"Connor...," her eyes watered and her bottom lip wobbled. Oh, great. "We were together for four years. How can you act like I don't mean anything to you?"

"You. Left. Me," I repeated slowly, trying not to raise my voice despite my blood pressure shooting through the roof. "I got over you because I had to, Vick. I moved on for my own survival."

"What if it was a mistake?" she whispered, blinking rapidly and sniffling. "What if I realized... I was wrong? That I threw away the best relationship I ever had?"

I lifted both shoulders in a shrug. "Not my problem, doll face." Damn it. I bit my tongue too late. My old nickname for her slipped out like a bad habit.

Her eyes widened upon hearing the name and her ruby lips parted to respond, but the door pushed open to make both of our heads turn. At the sight of Mel's raven black hair and big doe eyes, I felt simultaneous relief and dread in the pit of my stomach.

"Mel," I breathed, sitting back against my pillows again. "Hey."

Her eyes darted from me to Vicky, wide and full of questions. The temperature in the room seemed to drop a full ten degrees.

"Who are you?" she asked Vicky, the accusation already in her tone.

Oh shit. This would not end well.

I cleared my throat. "Mel, this is Vicky. She was my, ah..."

"Fiancee," Vicky so kindly finished my sentence for me.

"Ex-fiancee," I quickly corrected. "She was mistakenly

called here because of an outdated emergency contact form from when I was in the Marines." I stared hard at her, hoping I was finally making myself clear. "She was just leaving."

"No, Connor. I am *not* done talking to you," she reprimanded me like a stern mother. "Your little trailer park girl can wait."

I looked at her incredulously and, in that moment, my annoyance turned to pure loathing. "Oh no, you stupid bitch. How dare you?"

But it was too late. Mel was already backing out the door with tears in her eyes and taking jagged pieces of my heart with her.

"Mel, wait!" I yelled. "Babe, stop!"

She either didn't hear me or ignored me, walking as fast as she could back down the hall.

Vicky must have worn a smug look on her face, but I didn't spare her a glance as I jabbed the call button, not lifting my finger from it until a nurse came running and burst into my room.

"Is something wrong?" she asked.

"This woman needs to leave," I said, pointing at Vicky. "Call the police if you have to. I don't want her near me."

❧ 18 ❧

HUNTER

"So," I glanced at Razvan, hunched over like me in the waiting room while we allowed Mel and Connor to have some time together. "You two have made up, I take it?"

He lifted his gaze to me, smirking. "I guess you could say that."

"Just like that, huh? When I almost thought I had to fight you the other day?"

"I never would have fought you," he whispered. "She chose you over me at the time. I respect that. I was being a dick to her." He shrugged, rubbing his tattooed hands together. "I manned up and apologized. She did the same for her part. Now," his smirk grew wider. "I guess I'm part of the pack."

"We are quite the pack, aren't we?" I huffed out a laugh. "All pawing for attention from our alpha female."

"Yeah, you'd consider her an alpha?" Razvan's eyebrows lifted. "I'm not too brushed up on wolf hierarchies."

"It's in her, even if she doesn't know it yet," I answered.

137

"You see it in the way she steps into her ringmistress role. She thinks of it as an act, but that's really her. People just want to watch her, listen, and follow her lead. I bet the shaman powers have something to do with it, too. She's like a magnet and we can't fight the pull of her."

"Damn right," he muttered his agreement.

The moment he spoke, the waiting room door burst open. Mel flew through the room, right past us and toward the elevator.

Razvan and I sprung into action. He caught up to her first, grabbing her before the elevator opened.

"*Steluţa*, what is it?" He cradled her head against his chest and rubbed her back. "My little star, what happened in there?" From the muffled sounds, I realized she was sobbing.

I flattened my palm against her lower back and kissed the back of her head, not caring how close my face was to Razvan's.

"Sweet girl, please tell us," I murmured behind her ear. "We're here for you."

"*Her.*"

Our eyes followed where she peeked out from Raz's shirt, following an attractive blonde woman who just left the same waiting room and headed for the elevators. Her lip curled with disgust the moment she saw Mel sandwiched between me and Raz, then she turned her nose up and walked into the first one that opened.

Raz and I looked at each other, a mutual understanding passing between us. Connor either fucked up majorly or this was a perfect storm of misunderstanding.

"You go talk to him," Raz snarled protectively. "I might say something I regret. Plus, you know him better."

I nodded, placing a last kiss on Mel's head and squeezing her shoulder before I turned away. As I walked back toward the waiting room, the low murmurs of Raz speaking soothingly to her followed me.

A chuckle escaped me before I could help it. Could we be any more of a perfect yet fucked up balance? One guy hurt her, another comforted her, and another went to talk sense into the guy that hurt her.

Roo and Rinna, entranced by the toy set in the waiting room, didn't even notice the commotion around them.

"Guys, I'm going to talk to Mr. Connor real quick," I told them. "Stay here." I gave the command with an undertone of wolf growl so they knew I was serious.

"Yes, Dad," they answered.

I pushed through the door and stopped a nurse to ask for directions to Connor's room.

"Down the hall and to the left," she took in my towering frame nervously. "But um, he's not taking visitors right now. We're monitoring his blood pressure."

"It'll just be a minute," I gave her a wolfish smile, letting her know as kindly as I could that she did not want to get in my way. "Thank you."

Connor sat up in a hospital bed, with a blood pressure cuff around his arms and a nurse watching the machine. He looked fine, well, even. Just as disgruntled as usual. I pushed through his door without bothering to knock.

"You want to explain why Mel just ran out of here crying her eyes out?"

"Hey, no visitors!" the nurse snapped at me. "You need to leave."

"He's fine," Connor sighed. "You can leave us."

Her head snapped back to look at him, and he nodded,

urging her to go. She promptly unrolled the cuff from around his forearm and walked wide around me to leave the room.

"Well?" I prompted when we were alone.

"Because I couldn't get that stupid bitch out of here fast enough," he groaned, rubbing his hands down his face.

"Who's the stupid bitch?" I growled, remembering the way she looked at Mel before getting into the elevator.

"My ex," he sighed. "She wouldn't leave until I called nurses to get her the hell out. In that time, she called Mel trailer trash."

"Oh, no." I rubbed the back of my neck, knowing how sensitive Mel was about her past. "Fuck, Connor. Why was she here?"

"Apparently out of concern," he scoffed with an eye roll. "The hospital called her because she was my emergency contact. But I dunno, I think she was hoping to get money or some shit. Which I have none of."

I nodded. So a misunderstanding, then. Mel saw her in here and probably thought the worst. I couldn't blame her, and it definitely didn't minimize her hurt.

"Raz is with her?" Connor asked.

"Yeah."

"Good," Connor sighed, leaning back onto his pillows. "She needs you guys right now more than me."

"Con, it's not that big a deal," I sighed. "Yeah, she's hurt right now and we're here for her. But when she calms down and we explain, I'm sure she'll understand. You didn't want your ex to be here. I'm sure she knows that."

"Nah, you don't get it, Hunter," he shook his head. "Shit like this is why she needs you two. There is so much I can't control. This hospital visit is going to cripple me, pun not intended." He flashed a smirk before continuing. "I'll have to sell the RV just to pay for them checking my damn blood pressure. And the rest of this is going to be hanging over me for the rest of my life. I can't be a good partner to her if I can't even provide a roof over her head."

"Con, dude," I held up a hand. "There's no need to catastrophize this. Yeah, hospital bills suck ass, but Mel needs you too. We all stayed at Raz's last night. He's got plenty of room, I'm sure he'll take you in, too. We'll figure all that shit out."

"It's not just that, bro," Connor gave me a sad smile. "It's the PTSD. It's the bill collectors that are going to chase me forever. It's the fact that I'm going to be an ever bigger asshole to her now from being in constant pain because I can't get new legs that fit right. She deserves better."

"Con," I said after a long, uncomfortable silence. "She loves you, dude."

"And I love her. More than fucking anything. That's why I need to let her go." He laughed humorlessly. "God, I wish I met her first. I wish I put a ring on her finger, not Vicky's. Then we might have had a real shot at something."

I cleared my throat. "But she would have been like, fourteen right?"

Connor looked at me, then burst out laughing. "Yeah, you're right. It never would have worked. She made me happy for a brief moment in time, but it was never supposed to work."

"Connor, come on," I urged. "She will *never* give up on you, so why are you giving up on her? Fuck everything you can't control, just work on what you can. The four of us will look after each other, no matter what. Well six, if you include the kids."

"I can't risk it," he shook his head. "What if I get a flashback that's so bad and vivid, I hurt her? Or one of the kids? I've shot guns through walls before, Hunter, thinking I was back *there*. My nerve pain is only going to make it worse." He looked away, still shaking his head. "No, I can't risk hurting her or anyone, for that matter. I won't abuse the ones I love."

"Con," I choked out. "What exactly are you saying?"

"I'm saying," he growled. "Take your family. Take Mel and Raz, and move on. Leave me here and forget I exist."

19

MELODY

Raz or Hunter, usually both of them, held me every moment since running out of that hospital room. My face physically ached from crying so hard. My head pounded relentlessly, but their gentle caresses over my hair soothed me at least a little.

And then I thought of *her* sitting on the edge of Connor's bed like they had never been apart at all, and the tears flowed freely again. I was so wrapped up in my heart breaking, I barely noticed the guys leading me out of the hospital and back to the truck. Rinna crawled into my lap and wiped my tears away. I hugged her tight, grateful for her, but didn't want to burden her with my pain.

The next thing I knew, someone carried me from the truck. Lips kissed my forehead, and I just clung to this person's shirt and sobbed. The tattoos on the chest and neck told me it was Raz, but my brain seemed unable to form coherent thoughts. All I could picture was *them* together in an endless, unforgiving loop.

I was laid down in a bed, offered water and tissues,

then wrapped up snugly in blankets. All of these occurrences seemed to happen across a barrier, like I was in some kind of bubble disconnected from it all.

Eventually, exhaustion overtook me, and I succumbed to the darkness of sleep.

When I woke up, my eyes opened to meet a familiar black dragon gliding across the muscles of Raz's back. A long, pale arm wrapped around my waist from behind, holding me tightly. I broke eye contact with the inked dragon to turn around, meeting Hunter's sharp, golden eyes.

"Hey," he greeted softly, caressing over my back and ribs.

"Hi," I answered, my voice choked and raw.

"Do you need anything?" he lifted up to his elbow. "Food? Water? A hot bath?"

"Um," I rubbed my face, still tender and swollen. I must've looked like hell, too. "All of the above sound great, but where would I get a bath?"

The handsome wolf shot me a mischievous grin. "Turns out Raz has a tub that he hauls around when he travels. The guy likes his comforts on the road."

I let out a suppressed giggle. After seeing the Persian rugs, the knife collection, and the finest king-sized air mattress money could buy, it was clear that Raz enjoyed his luxuries.

"That's what I like to hear." Hunter stroked my face and kissed the bridge of my nose. "I love your laugh."

A shuddering sigh wracked through me. I didn't want to talk or think about what happened in the hospital. I already hurt too much and hoped Hunter wouldn't try to make me talk about it.

"Come on, let's get you in a bath," he pulled me gently toward the edge of the bed. "I'll get some food ready for you."

I followed him reluctantly out of bed and out of the tent. "That small tent," he pointed, "is where the bathtub is. It has its own propane heater and everything. Go ahead and soak," he kissed my forehead, "and I'll bring you food."

"Thank you," I murmured, leaning my head against him for a moment. Those two words couldn't even touch how grateful I felt for him and Raz.

"Of course." He gave me a final kiss and went to the main fire, where a large cast-iron pot sat on a grate above the flames.

The tub was small, although a perfect size for me, and looked to be made of a hard plastic. Probably easier to carry around that way. It was already filled with water, which felt comfortably warm to the touch. A folded towel, bars of soap, and a loofah had been placed on a wooden crate next to it.

I blinked away tears as I shed my clothing. The guys must have prepared this for me while I was sleeping. And that food smelled like it had been simmering for a while. What did I do to deserve thoughtfulness and care like this?

"Ahhh," I couldn't help but moan as I sank into the water, the heat enveloping me and sinking in my muscles like a full body massage. "You're a genius, Raz."

I leaned my head back to let my hair soak, the warmth on my scalp doing wonders for my headache. After soaking for a few moments, I picked up a bar of soap and began scrubbing it over my arms and chest.

"Mel?" Hunter scratched at the tent flap.

"Come in," I called.

His blush was adorable as he averted his eyes from me politely. While the edge of the tub just came over my shoulders, I had no bubbles to hide anything below the surface of the water.

"Is the temperature okay?" he asked, setting a bowl of stew next to the soaps. "Raz boiled the water a little while ago to purify it, then shut it off to cool down for whenever you were ready."

"It's perfect," I smiled. "Is he still asleep?"

Hunter nodded, laughing. "If I didn't know any better, I'd figure he was a cat shifter. That dude sleeps constantly."

"Reptiles sleep a lot too, don't they?" I asked, blowing on the stew to cool it. "Since they only eat like once a month."

"No idea," he grinned. "How's the food?"

"Delicious!" It really was. Although mostly meat and potatoes, I did find a few rogue vegetables as I spooned through the thick broth. So thoughtful for my human stomach. "Thank you, Hunter."

"Of course." He looked apprehensively toward the door. "Do you want me to leave you alone?"

"No," I answered. "Please stay. And you don't have to avoid looking at me, either." I playfully grabbed his chin and made him face me. "I figured you'd see me naked, eventually. It's only fair, right?" I laughed.

A grin widened across his face. "I just didn't want to be rude."

"You're the least rude person I've ever met," I told him. "These other two, on the other hand..."

He laughed with me, drifting his fingertips over the

wet skin of my arm and shoulder with the lightest ghost of a touch.

"Mel," he began in a more serious tone. "Do you want to talk about—"

I shook my head, cutting him off abruptly. "It's over. That's what he told you, right?"

His face fell, confirming my suspicion. Just as my heart felt like it stopped bleeding, the wound reopened again.

"How did you know?"

"I could just see it when they were in the room together." I swallowed a bite of stew, trying to distract the pit in my stomach. "It sounds stupid, but he didn't call me babe in front of her. And then when she called me tr—"

"Hey, no. You've got it all wrong." Hunter's gentle caresses on my arm turned into a desperate squeeze. "He was trying to make her leave, and she was being a stubborn bitch, that's all. He had nurses kick her out right after you left."

"Are you sure?" I searched his gaze, hope daring to grow within me.

"She means nothing to him, and you mean everything," he said, golden eyes locked on mine.

"But why did you say—"

"'Cause he's being a self-sacrificing idiot," Hunter sighed. "With no way to pay the hospital or get new prosthetics, he doesn't want to drag you down with him. He thinks the pain is going to make his flashbacks worse and he could seriously hurt you, or even the kids. So he wants you to move on."

"But..." Confusion swirled within me, bringing my headache right back. "You don't think he'd hurt me or the kids, do you?"

"Absolutely not, if he manages all his issues," Hunter replied. "But it sounds like he's given up on trying."

"We can't let him give up!" I stood from the tub, splashing water everywhere without giving a fuck. I grabbed the towel and started wiping myself dry.

"Mel, what are you doing?" Hunter didn't bother trying to hide looking at my naked body.

"I'm going back to the hospital to talk some sense into him." Grabbing his shoulder for support, I stepped out and continued drying myself off. "Before he does anything stupid."

"Hey, wait. Calm down." He took hold of my arms, now keeping his eyes glued to my face. "He's not going anywhere. They're still keeping him to watch his concussion. And you are still exhausted and emotional. Just take a breather, little fox."

"How could I not be?!" I demanded, raising my voice. "He's trying to break up with me over the stupidest, petty shit! I don't care about money or his flashbacks, I just want to be there for him. If he has no one, then he..."

"I know, I know." Hunter pulled me into his chest as I descended into body-wracking sobs again. He shushed me and stroked my hair, not caring that it was tangled or wet.

"You're incredible, you know?" he murmured against my forehead. "For caring so much. But it takes a lot of out of you, my sweet little fox. Take care of *you* for one night. Connor will be okay tomorrow. We'll see him when we can be calm and level-headed, okay?"

I nodded just as the tent flap rustled.

"Everything okay in there?" Raz called from the outside.

"Yeah," I sniffed, rubbing my face with my hands. "You can come in, Raz."

Wearing only his dark distressed jeans, Raz's fully inked torso moved like a living painting as he stepped into the tent.

"Ah, fuck! I'm sorry." He turned away the moment he saw that I was naked in Hunter's arms. "Didn't mean to interrupt."

"You're not," Hunter assured him with a dry laugh. "I told her what Connor said. She jumped out of the tub and was about to run back there buck ass naked."

"You shoulda let her," Razvan chuckled, still with his back turned. "Then we could chase her all the way down to the hospital and enjoy the view at the same time."

"You guys are the worst," I laughed, snuggling into Hunter's chest and returning the embrace that he wrapped around me. "This is just payback. Raz, did I tell about when I hugged a naked Hunter after the opening show?"

"No! How did that happen?"

As I retold the story, my awareness drifted to the heat and contours of Hunter's body. When I stepped in closer to squeeze him tighter, an unmistakable bulge pressed into my lower stomach. His breath hitched, and he stiffened, moving just a fraction of an inch away.

My own body ignited into a liquid heat, concentrating at my core. With Hunter pressed against me and Razvan's tattooed back watching me, thoughts entered my mind that I barely dared to voice.

I wouldn't let Connor set me free, or whatever supposedly noble way he tried to justify it. He wasn't perfect, and I accepted that about him. But I still needed him. And even if he didn't want to admit it, he needed me to keep his mind from going to dark places.

When he was low, these two lifted us back up. Sure, maybe just Connor and I would be too unstable and dysfunctional to make it together. But with the four of us? We were unbeatable.

"Razvan," I breathed in a sultry whisper while the full length of my body pressed against Hunter once again. "You don't have to turn around."

His head turned to the side, making the dragon on his back coil up as if ready to pounce on its prey. "Are you sure?"

"Please." My voice shook from either fear or anticipation. I couldn't tell which. "Look at me."

He turned slowly and his eyes heated immediately upon drinking in my curves, still wrapped in Hunter's embrace.

"You're beautiful, *steluţa,*" he murmured with genuine appreciation. "Conner and Hunter are lucky men."

"I feel way too overdressed," Hunter laughed in an attempt to lighten the thick tension growing in the room.

I slid my hands up his chest to wrap them around his neck. His touch drifted across my waist to my lower back, hovering just above my bare ass. An electrical intensity fired between us. I looked over to Razvan and felt the same intense chemistry from him.

Maybe it was selfish, but I didn't care anymore. For once, I wanted to forget about everything else and just feel good.

"I think both of you are overdressed."

✣ 20 ✣

MELODY

Neither of them said a word for a long moment, but Razvan seemed to get the idea first. A naughty grin spread across his face as he folded his arms across his chest.

"Have you ever been with two men before, *steluţa?*"

"No," I admitted, leaning my head against Hunter's chest. His heart pounded just as furiously as mine.

"Are you sure this is something you want to do?"

I reached out an arm to him. "Come here, Raz."

He approached me slowly, as if still trying to survey the situation. But when I cupped his face and pressed my mouth to his, he dropped all caution to the wind and kissed me back with pure, fiery passion.

His split tongue caressed both sides of mine, teasing my lips with playful flicks as he slid an arm across my upper back. When we parted, I stood on tiptoes and kissed Hunter in the next breath. He tensed in surprise but soon opened his mouth to me, too. From him I tasted that sweetness mixed with the alpha dominance that made me weak in the knees.

Just when I thought this couldn't get any hotter, Raz's split tongue danced along the back of my neck. He moved behind me, his jeans brushing against my ass as he kissed my neck, but not pushing against me. Yet.

"Now," I breathed when Hunter's kiss broke. "Did that bother either of you?"

"Not in the least," Raz whispered gruffly against my skin. "It's hot to see you kiss him, to see him wrapped around your beautiful body like this."

"Hunter?"

My pale wolf exhaled a deep breath and I could see he was trying to think with the correct head, to do the right thing by me.

"No, it doesn't bother me," he began. "I just don't want you to feel bad afterward if... this happens."

"I'm done feeling bad," I told him. "You two make me feel amazing and I just want more of that." I took his face in both of my hands. "Tomorrow, we're going to drag Connor out of a hellhole he's trying to bury himself in. But it'll be a ton of work and I can't do it by myself. I need you two with me. I need—"

He cut me off with a hard kiss, giving me every reassurance without words. As his tongue invaded my mouth, he dragged my hands down his body to stop at his pants. My fingers grazed the firm muscles of his abs before I flicked the button open, and he broke our kiss for just a moment to pull his shirt over his head.

Everyone's hesitation went out the window in that moment. Raz pulled my hips back toward him as his tongue danced along my spine. Hunter cupped my nape in a fiercely possessive hold as he captured my mouth again, all the gentleness gone and leaving only hot desire to take my breath away.

"Hey," Raz grazed his teeth along my ear. "Let's head back to the bedroom tent. Hunter, where are the little ones?"

"Home," he murmured gruffly. "At our den in the woods. They said they slept better there."

"Perfect," Raz hummed in a kiss against my shoulder. "My people have all left. No one should be around."

Hunter broke away from me to peek outside the tent. Shirtless and with his pants partially undone, he looked hot as sin and I nearly found myself salivating. He'd be right at home in a Calvin Klein ad.

"Coast is clear," he reported before stepping outside.

"Let's go, *steluţa*," Raz said with a playful swat to my ass.

With Hunter already out and Raz right behind me, I darted out of the tent, cackling with laughter. The bedroom was a quick jog away and I could have taken all the time in the world with no one else around, but it still felt naughty and thrilling being out in the woods without a lick of clothing on.

Hunter was waiting, leaning back on the messy air mattress on his elbows. "Hey, gorgeous," he greeted with a wide grin as my naked form approached him.

"Hello, handsome." I got the idea to crawl across the bed to him all slow and sexy, but that was quickly ruined by Razvan.

I screamed-laughed as the dragon shifter grabbed me around the waist from behind and picked me up. Despite my squirming, he easily carried me across the tent to the bed, where he dropped us both in a freefall.

"I was going to do a sexy walk and then crawl on the bed, but you ruined it," I laughed, wiping away tears.

"Oh well. Next time," the dragon grinned. "Preferably with me *and* Hunter on the bed."

"Fine," I sighed in mock disappointment, wriggling my way up the mattress to situate myself between them.

"It's the thought that counts." Hunter grabbed my waist and rolled me toward him, kissing me deeply to continue what we started.

I closed my eyes, sighing contently as I explored him with only the senses of touch and taste. His body, so tall and lean, seemed to have muscles that went on forever. I tried to count his abs as my fingers drifted down his torso, but he started kissing my neck, which was far too distracting for such a brain activity.

Behind me, Raz did the same exploratory touches across my back and waist. I never expected him to be so gentle while Hunter took control more aggressively. I thought they'd be the opposite.

Hunter and I finally worked his jeans down his legs and behind me, I heard the distinct unzip and rustling of Raz getting undressed. Giving Hunter one last kiss full of tongue and promise to return to him, I flipped over to face my tattooed dragon.

"Hi," I said shyly to those gray eyes filling my vision.

"Hello, *steluţa*," he returned, cupping my chin for a kiss.

A sharp thrill ran through me as the length of his body pressed again. This was so new to us. I'd gotten to know Hunter's body a little bit better since we spent more time together, but Razvan's was completely uncharted territory.

My fingers traced the art on his shoulders, his neck, his chest, and my lips soon followed. He groaned softly, caressing me as I took my time to explore. When I reached the waistband of his briefs, he stopped my hands.

"Before you go there," he rasped, "I want to say don't be alarmed and don't feel like you have to do anything." A playful grin twitched on his face. "I'm quite modified down there too."

"Now you've just made me curious," I giggled. After just a breath of hesitation, I dragged the edge of his underwear down. More tattoos decorated his hips and lower abs. In fact, they never seemed to stop as I slowly pulled the fabric even lower.

Turned out, they didn't.

My eyes widened as the black ink designs continued onto the shaft of his dick, decorating the thick organ with dot and line patterns like a monument. What was more, three metal balls pierced through the edge of his head just where it flared.

"Holy shit, Raz." The declaration came from Hunter looking over my shoulder, as I had been rendered speechless. "Do you get off on pain or something?"

"Nah. The pain of body mods is a rush, but it's not a sexual thing," he shrugged, his grin widening. "I just started to run out of real estate."

"What's next, your balls?"

"Yeah, probably," he remarked as casually as if he was talking about something as innocuous as a haircut. "Thinking of getting a Jacob's ladder too."

"What's that?" I asked, unsure if I really wanted to know.

"You sweet little thing," Raz teased me with a kiss. "It's

a set of surface piercings down the shaft of a dick." His face went serious at my shocked expression. "*Steluţa*, every dick piercing I get is with a woman's pleasure in mind. I've never had any complaints, but I realize it's strange to someone who's not used to them." He kissed me again with slow, deliberate sensuality, then pulled back with a smile. "If you want to just be with Hunter right now, I completely understand. I won't be offended."

"No, I just...," I swallowed and almost burst out laughing. The three of us were lying in bed, talking casually about Razvan's dick, which was sitting out proudly on display. "Will you show me what you like? I don't want to do anything wrong."

"Underneath all this ink, I'm a simple man, *steluţa*," he chuckled, nuzzling me. "Just being touched by you feels amazing. Do whatever you're comfortable with and I'll guide you if it's necessary."

I nodded, tilting my face up to kiss him again as my hands returned to his hips. He helped me slide his boxer briefs all the way down until I was no longer the only naked one. Dragging his mouth down my neck to nibble at my shoulder and collarbone, he pulled me forward and his hot shaft brushed across my belly.

I took the opportunity to look over my shoulder at Hunter. "Stop being so overdressed."

"Working on it," he laughed softly, kissing me as he slid his own boxers down. The treasure trail of pale blonde hair led from his navel down to a partially hard cock just as perfect and unblemished as the rest of him.

I had seen it before, when we were just "friends", but nothing stopped the full-body shudder of desire as he pressed against me. He let out soft growls as his hungry kisses traveled across my back, his cock thick and pulsing as it grew harder on my ass.

Sandwiched between Hunter and Raz, both of them kissing and touching me with a feverish need, their hips beginning to roll softly in alternating rhythms against my body, I never imagined I could be so lucky.

Sensations of pure pleasure overwhelmed me. I tried to touch them, to please them too, but they each just grabbed my hand and kissed it before returning to what they were doing—making me feel beyond incredible.

Raz made me cry out when his tongue teased my nipples into stiff, aching peaks. Hunter caressed my thighs until I was absolutely trembling before he touched my clit. I jerked back so suddenly, he groaned a curse and his cock twitched against my ass.

"May I?" Raz inched his hand down my lower belly. When I moaned a yes, his hand replaced Hunter's, who turned his attention to kneading my breasts as he nibbled my neck.

"Mm, you're so wet," Raz moaned against my lips as his hands caressed my folds. "I would love to taste you, steluţa."

Oh God.

Just the thought of that inhuman tongue pleasing me *down there* sent another surge of liquid heat through my core to coat his palm.

With a savage growl, he pinned my hips down toward the bed so I laid flat on my back. Hunter scooted up higher so that my head rested in his lap as Raz positioned himself between my legs. He kissed my mouth first, soft and sweet, but that smile was anything but sweet as he worked his way down my body.

His mouth left a trail of fire, traveling over every curve of me. He hummed against my skin, sending gentle vibrations to every sensitive part of my body. Hunter teased my nipples between his fingers as Raz made his way down, alternating between gentle and rough. By the time Raz reached my soaked, aching core, his magical tongue would barely have to do anything.

But still it did. He kissed my inner thighs, circling all around my center until I was begging and bucking my hips in his face. When his mouth finally pressed to my vulva, sparks flew across my vision. His tongue flicking against both sides of my clit made it feel like *two* men were pleasing me down there.

The wicked dragon still didn't let me come, though. He looked up at me from between my legs, eyes bright and full of mischief as he danced me around the edge, watching me moan and whine and thrash like a woman possessed.

I slid my head to the edge of Hunter's thigh and reached up, wrapping my fist around his cock. If Raz wouldn't let me get off, I'd find a distraction from the torture.

"Ohh, Mel," Hunter groaned as I stroked him, squeezing his pale flesh as my hand slid upward, just as Connor showed me. "Oh, that feels so good, little fox."

"Hunter, you're so fucking sexy... ahhhh!"

Raz pressed two fingers inside me, filling the aching emptiness as he stroked my top wall with those long, skilled fingers. His lips sealed around my clit as his tongue continued to stroke it with gradually increasing pressure.

"Do you feel good, beautiful?" Hunter pinched my nipples again, harder this time, making me cry out at the shared sensation between my nipples and clit. "Is this what you wanted?"

"This is better than what I ever wanted," I panted. "I've never felt sooo... oh God!"

Raz's tongue lashed my clit a final time before the orgasm crashed through me, hurtling me into a world of pleasure I didn't know was possible.

RAZVAN

She quivered so beautifully when she came apart, making the sweetest moans and whimpers when her gorgeous body thrashed.

I reluctantly pulled my mouth away from her pussy to let her recover and come back down as her release passed. Damn, she tasted divine, but I knew how sensitive women were after coming. Never wanting to leave, I kissed her thighs and the beautiful lines in her hips that led down to her pussy.

She shivered some more through her ragged breaths. Her cheeks flushed with pink as she gazed up at Hunter, who looked back at her like he treasured her above all else. He smoothed his hands down her body, palming her breasts and caressing her curves while she hummed in delight.

I only then noticed she had been stroking him and he was rock hard.

"Want to switch places, wolf?" I had a feeling Mel wouldn't want me fucking her first. On top of looking apprehensive about my piercings, I was wider than Hunter —not that his dick was small by any means. She also just knew him better than me.

"Gladly," he grinned, leaning down to suck those beautiful pink nipples before scooting around to the lower half of her body.

"Did you enjoy that, *steluța*?" I purred, lifting her head to set it in my lap like Hunter did.

"Is the sky blue?" she laughed, bringing her hands up to rake her fingers down my thighs. "You felt amazing. That tongue of yours is something else."

I hissed with pleasure at the resulting tingles of her nails on my quad muscles. My dick twitched, and I ached to be inside her. My dragon roared with the need to consume her, but I shoved him down. Only she would decide if she wanted me.

"The sky isn't actually blue," Hunter quipped as he settled between Mel's thighs. "It's just the reflection of the ocean."

Mel and I both groaned in unison. "So hot to hear you talk useless facts in bed," she teased, running her fingers through his platinum hair spilling over her skin. "That's something Connor would say..."

She fell silent, growing wistful, but Hunter brought her right back into the mood with us.

"When Con's back," he kissed the valley between her breasts, "he can be the trivia master while Raz and I rock your world."

She laughed, a light musical sound that wrapped around my heart and squeezed. I couldn't wait until Connor got his head out of his ass so we could make her laugh like that every day. She was beautiful to look at no matter what mood she was in, but seeing her face light up at a silly joke made her absolutely radiant.

Hunter smothered her mouth with a kiss, turning her giggles into soft moans as his hips lined up to hers. Her arms wrapped around his back, but she suddenly jerked away and broke off the kiss.

"Wait," she said, already panting again, and looked up at me. "Do you have condoms, Raz?"

"Ah, no." I rubbed my jaw, genuinely forgetting that humans used those things.

Her face turned red as it fell with disappointment. "Then I'm sorry guys, but I can't... I'm not on any birth control."

"Mel, shifters can't get humans pregnant," Hunter said softly. "It hasn't been scientifically proven, of course, but there's ah, lots of anecdotal evidence. And unless I'm mistaken," he glanced up at me. "We also don't transmit the same illnesses. Sexually or otherwise."

"What are you looking at me for?" I demanded in mock anger. "Just because I used to, ah, how would you say it, take sexual partners indiscriminately?"

"You could just say manwhore," Hunter snorted.

"Fine, yes. I used to manwhore. And I've never caught anything. Not even a cold."

"I don't think that's how that word is used," Mel giggled, gazing up at me. "But your accent is adorable."

"Ah yes, make fun of the foreigner," I growled, but smiled as I leaned down and peppered kisses all over her face and neck. Her laughs turned to hitched breaths and moans as I went from playful to sensual, nipping her skin where it was most sensitive until she arched against Hunter.

"Do you want to continue, little fox?" he asked, running his hands across her thighs, which had wrapped around his lean hips.

"Yes," she breathed, then whispered a word in his ear that made me instantly hard again. "Please."

He didn't need any further convincing. His hips rolled forward and Mel's face upon the moment of penetration was pure bliss.

"Ohhh," she moaned so hotly, balling her fists around the sheets already.

Hunter eased into her gently, making slow, careful thrusts as her body learned to accommodate him. He pushed himself up to straight arms, watching her move beneath him in wide-eyed awe as he built up to a steady rhythm.

"Raz," she moaned, making my cock ache. Somehow it was a huge ego boost that Hunter was the one fucking her and she was moaning my name.

"Yes, *steluţa?*" I stroked her hair, enjoying the glazed over look of pleasure on her face and the way her tits bounced as Hunter rutted into her.

"Do you want me to, ahh…," she trailed off in a wordless moan as Hunter changed up his rhythm, fucking her slow and deep.

"I want you to do whatever you want," I told her huskily. "I'll get my turn when you're ready."

She looked up at Hunter and tapped his arm. "Stop for a second?"

He obliged, pausing his thrusts and pulled out to sit kneeling between her legs. "You okay?" he panted, his breaths already heavy. Coated in her juices, his cock hung taut and rock hard between his thighs. I found myself licking my lips.

I highly preferred women, but every once in a while, another man caught my eye. Anyone with a pulse could see how attractive Hunter was. His pale, unmarked skin didn't need a drop of ink to look sexy. His tall, athletic figure with that long, perfect cock to match. And I loved how Mel tasted so much, I wouldn't be opposed to licking her off him...

"Mmm!" A soft tongue flicking underneath my cock head brought me out of my fantasies and back to reality, and *oh*, what a reality it was.

Mel had flipped over to her hands and knees. Her big, chocolate eyes gazed up at me as she hesitantly took me into her mouth. My heart soared and my cock stiffened to stone. She wanted to pleasure me, but still felt unsure of herself. Behind her, Hunter smoothed his hands over her back and perfect, perky ass before lining up to fuck her again.

"Yes, *steluţa*," I hissed as her lips descended over my entire head. Her teeth clicked against my piercings, but it only heightened my pleasure. "Just like that. Yes."

Growing more confident with my praise, she took more of me and let out a moan that vibrated over the metal balls, tingling all the way down to *my* balls. Hunter had entered her again and thrust slowly to not jostle her too much while she sucked me. His jaw tensed and I could practically see his teeth gritting. He was dying to fuck her brains out, to take her like the animal he was, but held back to keep her comfortable.

Just like him, I clenched my fists around the sheets at

my sides, fighting everything in me to not fuck her gorgeous face until I exploded at the back of her throat. With every thrust from Hunter, her moans grew louder and uninhibited. She took me deeper down her throat with no assistance, no longer bothered by my piercings. The pressure from her mouth on them just enhanced my own pleasure.

"Fuck, *steluţa*," I groaned, unable to keep my hands off her. I reached under to pinch her nipples, making her squeals even louder and more erratic. Hunter started grunting and growling as he pounded into her more forcefully, reaching around her thighs to strum her clit as he fucked her.

The sight of her next orgasm quaking over her body sent me spilling deep into her mouth. Letting out a string of curses as I released violently, I heard Hunter doing the same as he came too.

The poor girl could barely stay up on her hands and knees as the pleasure rocked through her, but she pushed farther down my shaft to swallow every drop. I didn't even realize my hands tangled in her hair, pulling her down on my cock until she patted my thigh to let her up.

"Sorry! Are you okay?" I rasped, my pulse pounding in my ears.

"More than okay," she smiled dreamily, resting her head on my thigh as she collapsed down on the mattress with Hunter laying out beside her.

"You are incredible," he murmured, his own skin flushed pink as he wrapped an arm around her waist and poured kisses over her back and shoulders.

I scooted down to recline next to them, resting my hand on her hip as it gently rose and fell with her breaths.

"Enjoy yourself?" I drawled with a lazy smile. Her

bright eyes and flushed face told me all I needed to know, but I wanted to hear her say it.

"Very much." She rolled onto her belly and scooted toward me to lay her head on my chest. The gesture took me aback. Women never wanted to cuddle with me. They wanted me to fuck them senseless, to come under my magical tongue, maybe suck my dick as a half-hearted reciprocation, but they never curled up next to me like this.

"Did you enjoy yourself?" Mel looked up at me from laying over my heart. "I didn't hurt your piercings or anything, did I?"

"Is water wet?" I grinned down at her, stroking her hair out of her face. "You could never hurt me, *steluţa*. And even if you did, I'm sure I'd still enjoy it."

"Oh really?" she playfully closed her teeth over my nipple. "I like a little pain too."

"Do you now?" Hunter piped up from the other side of her. "Like what?"

She blushed as she lifted her head to look over her shoulder at him. "Connor has, um, spanked me. And I got really into it one time."

"You should have mentioned it while I was behind you," he teased, nuzzling her neck as he groped the perky globes of her ass.

"I did, but my mouth was full!"

The three of us laughed, relaxed and comfortable in post-orgasmic bliss. In my experience, all threesomes were different. Some were more comfortable after doing the deed, some were awkward as hell. But none had ever felt this... *natural*. It was almost unsettling how normal this felt. Mel's fingers traced my tattoos as she chatted with me and Hunter, my arm around her back and his hand drifting across her leg and hip. It just felt so... cozy and secure.

I caught Hunter's eyes a few times looking across Mel and over to my body, reclined and stretched out with our girl snuggled under my arm. My heart quickened when I noticed it, but his eyes quickly darted back to Mel, kissing her arm or somewhere as he stared at her adoringly.

Maybe it didn't mean anything. His mind could have just been wandering, but if there was a chance he was sometimes into men too...

The thought both aroused me and filled me with dread. How would Mel feel about that? This was the south, after all. They were almost as bad as Romania when it came to same-sex unions. Of course, I wouldn't act on anything without her full knowledge and consent. And if it made her the slightest bit uncomfortable, that was enough for me to never act on it. But if there was a chance she was okay with it during any future threesomes...

"Hey," she grinned at me wickedly, sliding a hand down my torso. "Looks like you're getting excited again."

MELODY

Raz's mouth spread into a cocky grin. "Just thinking about all the ways I could give you pleasurable pain, *steluţa*."

"You're thinking about something, I can see," I teased, trailing my hand down past his shaft to cup his heavy balls. He groaned as I massaged them in my palm, his pierced dick flexing as it grew harder.

"I'm good for another round." Hunter's mouth was hot against my ear, his teeth trailing along the shell of it. As he shifted his weight behind me, his semi-hard cock pressed against my ass.

"What am I going to do with you two *and* Connor?" I moaned as Raz pressed hot, sensual kisses underneath my jaw. "If we keep this up, I'll never be able to walk."

"Then we'll carry you," Raz growled against my skin. "Preferably while still on one of our dicks."

"Or both of our dicks," Hunter added. His hands palmed my ass cheeks apart, leaving no question as to what he implied.

I shivered against him, both with desire and nervousness. "I've never done that before," the confession escaped my lips.

He kissed me reassuringly. "Another time then, but not now."

"What *would* you like to do now, *steluța?*" Raz murmured as he made a trail of hot kisses down my neck. "Now that you've got me by the balls."

I giggled, releasing him there to stroke his shaft. He groaned against my neck, his cock hardening in my fist with every passing second.

"I want to... be with you," I muttered, somehow still feeling shy despite what just happened between the three of us.

He pulled away from my neck, looking at me with surprise and then delight. "Why don't you climb on top," he said in a husky whisper. "So you can be in control."

I nodded, throwing my leg over to straddle him. Still soaked from the first session, I wouldn't need much warming up. His shaft pressed against the tender folds of my vulva as I started to move against him, unsure if I was teasing myself or him more.

"Fuck, that's hot," Hunter mumbled. He propped himself on one elbow and stroked himself with the other hand. Hot, greedy need surged through me as I watched him. I'd make sure not to leave him out.

My tattooed dragon growled hot curses as I slid my pussy back and forth on his shaft, bracing my hands on his chest. He pushed himself to sit up, his back against the rigid support of the tent, and grabbed my head to claim my mouth in a kiss.

Right away, this felt different. Yes, he kissed me with

just as much passion, and that wonderful tongue stroked the inside of my mouth in a hot, delicious caress. But I felt something else, like his feelings for me poured from his mouth to mine. It stole my breath away, and I gasped, kissing him again and again to chase that feeling.

Somehow I knew he was giving me something he never gave anyone else, despite surely kissing and fucking hundreds of women. The aloof, former manwhore dragon made love to me with his mouth.

"I take back what I said before. *That* was hot." Hunter's voice filtered back into my consciousness. When I looked over at him, his cock already glistened with pre-cum. His sexy abs flexed with each short breath he took, already straining to hold himself back.

"You gonna sit there and provide commentary while you jerk off like a creep, or you gonna join us?" Raz flashed a smile. I couldn't help but notice his eyes dilate even more as he watched Hunter stroke himself.

"I'm content to watch for now," Hunter returned his grin lazily. "I'll cut in when she needs a break."

"Promise I won't leave you out," I winked at him before sliding up to let Raz's wide head kiss my entrance.

He wrapped a hand around the base for me, holding himself steady as I slowly lowered my hips.

"Ahhh." A harsh breath escaped me as my pussy stretched around him. How was I able to take so much of him in my mouth? His thickness pressed against all my inner walls with no room to spare. His piercings just inside of me rubbed in an intense but not unpleasant way.

"Take your time," he murmured, moving his hands to my waist to keep me elevated.

"I might need a minute," I panted sheepishly.

"Of course, *steluţa*." His smile up at me from the mattress bordered on cocky, but the warmth radiating from him calmed my nerves. Sure, he knew how big he was and couldn't help that. But he'd never want to hurt me.

A kiss on my shoulder drew my attention away for a moment. Hunter settled behind me, straddling Raz's legs and his own erection propped up against my ass. His arms slid around to cup my breasts, rolling my nipples between his fingers as he nuzzled my neck.

"Raz's hands look full so I'm helping you relax," he said, a smile in his voice. "Raz, do you mind me back here?"

"Not at all." Raz's voice was low and throaty. His eyes flickered from Hunter back to me. "Anything to keep our girl comfortable."

"You guys are the best," I sighed, arching back against Hunter as his hands sailed across my body. "What would I do without you?"

"That's not something you ever have to worry about." I felt his wolfish grin against my neck. "You're our shaman. You're stuck with us."

The retort in my throat came out a strangled moan as Hunter kissed me savagely, one fist in my hair and his other palm skimming down my belly to work my clit.

Inch by inch, I seated myself down on Razvan. His head tipped back with a groan as I lowered myself all the way, my breaths short as he filled me so utterly and completely. He dug his fingers into my hips with an iron grip, like I was his last anchor for control.

My movements started out slow and measured, just testing out the sensations of his piercings pressing into my top wall. With him guiding my hips, I found myself clutching his fingers for dear life. Every lift and lower of my body sent me chasing the most intense sensations and I couldn't get enough.

"Yes," Raz hissed between grunts and groans. "God, you feel amazing."

I leaned forward, bracing my forearms on his chest to kiss him. God, kissing him was like an addiction. Especially since that last one. He pulled me down further the moment our lips met. With our chests pressed against each other, it was a moment of just us.

His kisses were tender as he cupped my face, looking into my eyes as he began rolling his hips up to meet mine. The way he touched me, looked at me, kissed me, was so intimate it almost brought tears to my eyes. I never felt like this, not even with Connor. It was every bit as intense as his thick cock driving in and out of me, his piercings adding an extra layer of sensation as they stroked my channel.

Smack!

"Ahh!" My right ass cheek stung as I turned to look back at Hunter, who grinned impishly. "What was that for?"

"You said you liked spanking," he shrugged.

Raz shook with laughter underneath me. "She does. I felt her tighten around me when you did that."

They were right. The light sting of pain just amplified the pleasure surging through me. I felt like I walked along a razor's edge, the border of pleasure and pain.

"Want more?" Hunter rubbed his hands together as I returned upright.

"Yes," I sighed, bracing my hands on Raz's chest again. "Yes, please."

"So fucking hot to hear you say that," my dragon growled, driving his hips more forcefully to match me thrust for thrust. "I love hearing you ask for more."

The ability to form words escaped me as he filled and emptied me relentlessly. Hunter's smacks on my ass behind me sent electrified tingles to my nipples and clit. Raz's thumb stroked over that pleasure button just as my breaths grew shorter, my moans erratic and frenzied. That razor's edge was seconds away from cutting me apart, releasing everything I held back.

The combination of everything—Raz's thick cock, his piercings, his hand on my clit, and Hunter's teeth in my shoulder, sent me hurtling over the edge. Raz flexed hard inside me, spilling warmth as he roared and clutched at the sheets like a lifeline.

"Little fox," Hunter rasped in my ear. "I'm so close. Where do you want me, beautiful?"

I turned around, exhausted, panting, and still drunk off my orgasm. I lifted off of Raz, pushed Hunter down and climbed on to straddle him.

"Holy... fuck," he moaned the moment I impaled myself on him.

I rode him like a woman possessed, crashing my hips down as I chased the pleasure relentlessly. My orgasm from Raz never truly finished, and quickly began building into another.

"Yes, use me," Hunter rasped, gripping my hips much like Raz had. "Fuck me. Take what you need."

The scream tore from my throat as I came again just moments later. Hunter's cock seemed to press all new buttons, stroking inside me in a different way than Raz had. My control was no match for the previous pleasure combined with new sensations. I drowned in all of it, and happily. Hunter's release only extended my pleasure, which still felt over too soon.

The next sensations coming over me were the soft sheets, a pillow under my head, and warm bodies on either side of me. Two pairs of lips kissed me in various places. Raz's tongue tickled my earlobe, making me giggle and squirm. The last thing I heard was the chuckle from his chest, a soft rumble like thunder, before sleep overtook me.

❧ 23 ❧

MELODY

I woke up alone, delicious soreness in my body as a reminder of last night. Smiling, I stretched, taking up the entire king-sized mattress as I spread my arms and legs wide. The last few days had been exhausting. For the first time in what felt like ages, I felt truly relaxed and well-rested.

Raz sat facing the fire when I dressed and left the tent, turning to grin at me as I sat next to him.

"Hello, sleeping *steluţa,*" he greeted with a kiss on my cheek.

"Hi," I leaned my head on his shoulder. "How long have I been out?"

"Ten hours or so. You might be just as hard a sleeper as me," he teased.

"I really needed that," I murmured, running a hand through my hair. "I feel actually awake for the first time in days."

"You needed the sleep or what happened before?"

"Both." I pressed a kiss to his cocky grin, welcoming

the caress of a tongue on my lip. I would never get tired of feeling that.

"Where's Hunter?" I asked.

"Checking on the kids." His voice grew soft as he looked away from me and at the fire. "He'll be back shortly."

I wrestled with the thought of asking him about what I noticed between them. His lustful looks at Hunter, and the way they just seemed so comfortable with each other. Should I ask Hunter first? Maybe in my own lust-filled haze, I was just imagining things?

"What?" I said to Raz's playful nudge to my elbow.

"I said," he smirked, "when do you want to go see Connor?"

"As soon as possible," I answered. "I just hope we don't run into that bitch again."

"I don't think she'll be a problem," he offered. "And if she does show up, Hunter and I will take care of her."

"That's my boys." I looped my arm through his, gazing at the flames which he undoubtedly created. I thought back to when he lit Connor's campfire with just a quick exhale of breath. I thought it was a magic trick at first. Although no trick, my dragon was definitely magical.

"If you don't mind waiting until nightfall," Raz said. "I can fly us there if you'd like. It'll be faster."

"Really?" I lifted my head. "You want me to ride you?"

"Well, always, as long as you moan so pretty like you did." He laughed when I smacked his arm. "Of course I do, *steluţa*. I'd love to show you my perspective when I go on my night flights."

"It just feels a little weird to me," I admitted. "I mean, if humans knew what you were, they'd exploit you for that.

You'd be like those poor horses pulling carriages around for tourists."

"I know," he said solemnly. "They'd use me for that and much worse. Think of what the Pentagon would do if they got ahold of a dragon."

"Jesus," I muttered in disgust. "You'd be a perfect weapon to them."

"Right," he agreed. "But I don't mind being your personal taxi. I trust you, steluţa."

"And I trust you," I returned, lacing my fingers through his. "Completely. I won't ask you about other women anymore and... I'm sorry I assumed so much about you."

"You already apologized for that." He kissed my forehead. "It's in the past now. And..." He hesitated, his throat moving as he swallowed. The words seemed to fight their way from his mouth.

"Thank you for trusting me."

I snuggled closer to him, pulling his arm around me so I could nestle into his side. Even through his leather vest, I felt his heart racing. Trust was a big thing for him, and I'd be sure to treasure it. I still didn't know much about him, like why he had such a fragile relationship with trust and why he remained in the carnival at all. But with time, we'd get to know each other.

Just last night, even though it was sex, and hot sex at that, I could feel him open up to me on a deeper level. Some kind of channel opened between us, connecting us through the intimacy we shared and even now, just sitting together in front of a fire. It felt like the intangible parts of me and him molded together into some kind of oneness.

"Hungry?" he murmured into my hair.

"Starving," I admitted.

"You're gonna have to wait for Hunter for that," he cracked, poking me in the ribs. "He's the master chef around here."

"You ass," I groaned, moving to jab him back before he caught my fingers with a lightning fast hand.

We fell into some comfortable domestic tasks while waiting for Hunter. Raz polished his knives before packing them away carefully. I shook out the sheets and blankets on the bed, then carefully folded them despite his teasing they would get messed up again soon.

I heard Roo and Rinna talking excitedly before I ever saw the wolf family returning through the woods. The pups squealed when they saw me and ran, attaching firmly to each of my legs.

"Hey guys!" I laughed, groaning and struggling to walk as they giggled at my plight.

"I ate a caterpillar. It was nasty!" Roo declared, wrapping his lanky arms and legs around me even tighter.

"I bet it was, dude."

Hunter caught up a few steps later, carrying a large cooler with our food in it, no doubt.

"Hey you." My heart fluttered at seeing his biceps taut and flexed under the weight of the cooler. Even while carrying supplies, he looked sexy as hell. I tilted my chin up for a kiss, smiling at him but unable to stand on tiptoes thanks to my new child leg weights.

"Hey." To my surprise, he bypassed my mouth and brushed his lips against my cheek in something barely resembling a kiss. It was how I kissed my mom when she drunkenly insisted on it, and I wanted to do anything but touch her.

I blinked, stunned at his sudden coldness when we'd been so close just hours ago. He *never* did this hot and cold thing like Connor. Ever since the day we met, he'd been slowly escalating his affection toward me. And now, after sleeping with me, he just flipped and did the opposite?

Razvan noticed too, lifting an eyebrow as Hunter began setting skewers of meat over the fire without so much as a hello to him. The only ones who seemed oblivious were the kids, still wrapped around my legs like monkeys on tree trunks.

"Walk with us, Mel! You can do it!" Rinna yelled.

"Urgh, I dunno. You guys are too big." I took a couple half-hearted steps, grateful for the distraction.

"Leave Mel alone," Hunter snapped. "Come over here and eat. Then you two can play."

They reluctantly detached from me and shuffled over to the fire, knowing better than to disobey their father's tone. I hurried into Raz's main tent, deciding to look for eating utensils and get some distance from the sudden tension.

"Hey," Raz followed hot on my heels and grabbed my arm as soon as we entered the tent. "Whatever's crawled up his furry wolf ass has nothing to do with you. I promise, steluţa."

"You don't know that," I muttered, distractedly rummaging through the shelves for plates or bowls, until he took both of my arms and made me face him.

"I do know," he insisted, his face softening. "I saw the way he looked at you last night. I saw how badly he wanted to please you and how tightly he held you while you slept. I don't know what's up with the sudden change, but I know for a fact that you give him solace from everything that's happened to him." His voice lowered, as did his eyes, to the ground. "Just like you do for me."

"I don't know, Raz. I..." my voice choked, Hunter's cold approach toward me playing on a loop in my head like a form of self-mutilation. "I can handle Connor throwing up smoke and mirrors because it's how he protects himself. I can find my way through the fog of his mental illness and find the real him. But him *and* Hunter doing this? I can't, Raz. I just can't..."

"Shhh," Raz pulled me into his chest, stroking my hair and back. "That's not what this is, I'm sure of it. He's a single dad, remember? The kids are probably on his last nerve and pissing him off. He's allowed to feel frustrated with them, just give him space."

"I hope you're right," I sighed into his chest, although I couldn't keep the doubt from creeping into my voice.

"Trust him like you do me," he murmured. "He's not perfect. None of us are. He'll come back to you when he's ready. If not, he's a bigger idiot than Connor."

I chuckled, despite myself. We still had to convince Connor to come back to me, and that alone left a painful bruise on my heart.

With a sweet kiss and a few more reassuring words, Raz and I left the tent and headed back toward the capital of Awkward Central. Hunter pointedly ignored us, staring intently at the skewers as he carefully turned them over the fire or muttering a few words to his kids who sat angelically beside him.

Raz cleared his throat, settling on a log across the fire from Hunter.

"We're thinking of going back to Connor tonight,

when it's dark," he began. "I'll shift so Mel can ride me. You all can shift and meet us there if you'd like."

"Sure, that sounds fine," Hunter muttered unceremoniously, still not looking at either of us. "Food's done. Come and get it."

"Are you eating with us?" I asked, disappointment creeping into my voice as I watched him stand and shed his clothing. He was being so standoffish I couldn't even enjoy looking at him naked.

"I already ate," he said flatly, folding his clothes into a neat bundle. "I'm going for a run. I'll be back before nightfall."

Without another word, the sounds of joints popping and organs rearranging echoed through the trees. Hunter fell to all fours, the snowy white fur covering him last. And in the next instant, he was a white blur racing through the brush.

24

MELODY

"Ready?"

I nodded, taking my tenth glance around to make sure we were truly alone.

"No one else is here, *steluţa*," Raz chuckled as he shed his clothing. "Trust me, I could hear, see, and smell them from miles away."

Moonlight turned his bare skin a silvery hue, making his tattoos look even more magical and enigmatic. I leaned back against the tree, taking in every sleek, liquid movement of his ink as he peeled away his clothing. When he finally stripped completely naked, my core clenched around nothing, remembering how thickly he filled me and how his piercings felt.

"Like what you see?" he grinned smugly. Of course he knew the answer to that.

"Nah," I joked, unzipping the backpack I held for his clothes. "But if you hang out naked more often, I might come around to you."

"Uh-huh," he chuckled, folding up his clothes and

placing them inside the backpack, which I then zipped closed and slid my arms through the straps.

"Ready when you are, naked tattooed man with a killer body and amazing dick who is totally not my type."

He cupped my chin, grinning. His eyes looked like liquid metal in the moonlight. "A kiss before we go, since I won't be able to for a whole minute."

My grin matched his as I tilted my face up, our lips melding in a smooth, passionate dance that I wished never had to end. I grabbed the back of his head to kiss him harder and felt his heart beating against mine.

Holy shit, I'm totally smitten with him, I realized. Just looking at him or hearing his voice put a big stupid smile on my face. It was similar to the nervous giddiness I felt when Hunter and I started getting close, before he went from a warm, caring puppy of a man to a cold, solid brick wall.

Like earlier in the day, he barely said a word when he got back from his run. He puttered around the campsite until dusk fell, then headed for the hospital with the kids since it would take longer for them to reach there on four legs.

Recalling his behavior that day only made me kiss Razvan harder. Now that two of my men had become moody assholes, he was the one consistency in my life. He reassured me when Hunter's behavior stung, and here he was now, holding me under a full moon and kissing me like he never wanted this to end, either.

Never in a million years would I have believed I'd start falling for the arrogant, tattooed Romanian who sampled women like free snacks at the carnival. And I never thought he'd be such a rock, a point of stability when everything else seemed to fall apart.

"Do you want to see your other man or not?" he teased when we broke apart breathlessly, kissing my nose.

"You make it very tempting to say not," I sighed. "But yes, let's go."

He nodded, placing a final peck on my lips before stepping away to shift.

At first, it looked like all his tattoos filled in to make his skin completely solid black. Then a shiny white glare reflected the moonlight as his skin turned to solid dragon scales. At the same time, I heard the same sickening pops and cracks as his skeleton rearranged itself and grew to ten times the size of a man.

Within a minute, a massive black dragon stood before me. It was no less wondrous and awe-inspiring than the first time. Razvan stretched his wings, snorting tendrils of smoke before folding them against his back again.

"God, you're magnificent," I whispered, approaching him.

He leaned his large, reptilian nose against my palm and let out a low, rumbling growl like a purr against my hand. Those metallic gray eyes were exactly the same and looked at me with the same warmth and affection as human Razvan.

"I probably should have asked the best way to get on you," I realized aloud, taking in the bumps, ridges and spikes that adorned his body.

He let out a series of huffs that could only be laughter before lowering his belly to the ground. He laid there like a loafing cat, looking at me expectantly. If only there was some way to communicate.

Running my hand down his neck and along his back, I decided to just climb aboard and see what happened. Grabbing a spike along his backbone, I braced one foot against his ribs and threw the other over.

"Hang on," I told him when he started to fidget underneath me. "Trying to not stab myself in the vagina here."

That only made him shake even more as he repeated that dragon laugh. Finally, I settled over where the spikes smoothed out into ridges. It wouldn't be the most comfortable ride, but at least I wouldn't get stabbed and not be able to enjoy that dick of his anymore.

Yes, because that's the worst that can happen when you get a dragon spike through the pussy.

"Okay," I told him. "I think I'm ready."

I was not ready.

He pushed off the ground so fast, I lurched backwards and almost lost control. I couldn't stop the scream that tore from my throat as we ascended high and fast above the treetops. I squeezed around him with my knees and held onto his neck for dear life. And somewhere under my gripping fear of falling off and dying, my brain tried to wrap around the fact that I was *riding a fucking dragon.*

I couldn't catch my breath until he leveled out, beating his massive wings at a leisurely pace. I was still scared for my life, but the beauty of our surroundings put me at ease.

The moon hung so full and bright, I felt like I could reach out and touch it. Trees passed under us like they were children's toys. Around me I could see the shapes of the hills and winding roads you could never see from on the ground. I had never been on a plane before, but I could only imagine it didn't feel nearly as free as this.

"Raz, this is amazing," I whispered, unsure if he could

hear me through the wind whipping past us. "*You're amaz-ing.*" I ran my hands across his black scales like obsidian. They gave off a pleasant warmth—higher than body heat but not quite burning.

I closed my eyes just to feel the sensation of him carrying me. The air felt cool and fresh up here, his body solid underneath me. He wouldn't let me fall. On a whim, I took my focus inward. I shut out the wind whipping past my ears and listened for the dragon, the one on his back that seemed to move through me when I touched his back in bed.

I felt the heat of its flames licking the air, its powerful body wrapping around me, but this felt different. Rather than more scales and fire, this presence felt like a man wrapping around me. Strong, human arms I could practically feel encircling my waist, along with human lips and a tongue kissing my neck. A tongue split down the middle.

Razvan?

Steluța?

Hearing his voice, his *human* voice, startled me so badly I nearly lost my balance and the connection we held.

You can hear me? I thought.

Yes. You can hear me?

Yes! How is this happening? Where are you? I mean, I know I'm riding the dragon-you, but where are you-you?

I'm in the dragon, he replied. He is in control and I'm in the backseat, to put it simply. My consciousness is still here, but my human form is dormant, basically. Until I choose to change back.

So I'm talking to you telepathically? This is so weird!

I guess, his mental voice laughed. This must be another one of your shaman abilities.

Right. I'd been so consumed by Connor's fall, I forgot

to see Thembi again. The carnival had broken down for the season and she was surely gone by now. Like everything else, I'd have to figure this out on my own.

Have you talked like this to others before?

Never, Raz answered. *You're the first.*

This is... wild. I thought. *I must be able to talk to Hunter this way, too.*

Probably. Although I wouldn't attempt it right away.

You're right, I agreed. *Not until he comes and talks to me using his damn mouth.*

That's my girl. I didn't miss the pride in his voice. *We're coming up on the hospital now. I'm landing a bit farther away so we don't get seen.*

He overshot the hospital, which looked like a big white Lego block passing underneath us, and landed in a wooded area just beyond the parking lot.

"Do I have to give these back to you?" I whined when Raz shifted back to human and held his hand out for the backpack of clothes.

"Not unless you want me locked up in the mental ward," he grinned, playfully snatching it from me.

His demeanor immediately changed as he started getting dressed. He grew quiet, and the smile went away. He didn't look at me once as he shrugged on his clothes.

"Is something wrong?" I asked.

"No, why?" he muttered, propping his foot up on a bench to lace up his motorcycle boots. Still, he didn't look at me.

"Not you, too," I pleaded. "Hunter and Connor are one thing, but I can't handle all three of you being weird around me."

"I'm not—I'm sorry." He put his foot down and took a

deep breath, looking at the sky. "I'm just wrapping my head around the mind-speaking thing. I didn't even know that was possible."

"Me neither," I whispered. "Thembi never mentioned it. But I see it as a good thing. We can still talk while you're in shifter form."

He nodded his agreement but still looked apprehensive.

"What? Is there something else?"

"*Steluța*, could you... see anything?" His face hardened, his sharp eyes on mine. "If you can talk to me with your mind, can you also *see* what's in my mind? Or know what I'm thinking or feeling that's not in words?"

"I—I don't think so," I rubbed my forehead. "When you were laying in bed, and I touched the tattoo on your back, I could feel like your dragon was in the room with me. I felt his fire, his scales, and like his body wrapped around me. But just now, it was the opposite. I felt *you*, Razvan, like the human part of you was with me."

He nodded again as he listened, then grabbed my hand as we walked together toward the hospital.

"Forgive me for mentioning it, but there are things about me I'm not ready to talk about." He brought my palm to his lips and kissed it. "You'll probably find out eventually, but now isn't the time."

"It's okay. There's stuff in my past you don't know about, either," I slid my arm through his, wanting to touch more of him. "Although you do know a big chunk of it."

"As you do of mine," he said with a kiss to my temple.

We walked on in comfortable silence until we came around the front of the hospital, where we met Hunter and the kids already in human form. Hunter nodded at us, the barest of greetings, before turning to head inside with his family.

Raz muttered some insult under his breath, and I rubbed his arm as we followed the wolf family inside. This late at night, most of the lights were off and the hospital was nearly empty. Only a single security guard took notice of us as we headed toward the elevators.

"Excuse me, can I help y'all?" he asked, lumbering toward us.

"We know where we're going, thank you." I flashed him a smile as I hurried into the elevator, standing closer to Hunter than I intended.

"Folks, there are no visitors at this hour. You'll have to come back—"

Razvan turned and placed a hand on the man's chest, a final warning for him to stop.

"We'll be quick. And we won't steal anything. Promise." He flashed a smile, then jumped in the elevator as the man blinked dumbfoundedly.

"What was that?" I asked him on our way up.

"Old trick my grandmother taught me," he answered. "A type of hypnosis. Supposedly a talent unique to Romanian people."

"I knew it. You're a vampire, too," I teased.

He snorted with laughter while the kids giggled and playfully bit each other. Hunter remained still as a stone.

Connor's floor was equally empty and dark as the ground floor of the hospital.

"I think I want to talk to him alone," I whispered. "At first."

"We'll still come in and back you up," Raz answered.

"There's probably night shift nurses who will try to stop you. Right, Hunter?"

The wolf grunted an affirmative, and I fought back the urge to snap at him. I did not need his moodiness right now, especially when I was about to be dealing with Connor's.

Sure enough, two nurses looked up the moment we opened the door from the waiting room.

"Excuse me, there's no visitors—"

"Ah, Marni! So good to see you again." Razvan squeezed my hand before shooting a charming smile at the nurse. "I've been thinking about you ever since that night. Why haven't you called?"

"Um, it's Elena. I'm sorry, but do I know you…"

I was already down the hall and rolled my eyes when I turned the corner to Connor's room. To my own surprise, I didn't feel an ounce of jealousy at Raz flirting with the nurse. He was doing nothing more than causing a distraction, and that man knew well how distracting he could be.

My feet slowed to a stop outside Connor's room. His main light was off, but he was awake. He laid back on his pillows, eyes open and bluish light flickering on his face. It took me a moment to realize it was a TV.

Steeling myself with a deep breath, I pushed his door open and let myself inside. His head lifted up at first with surprise, then a dry smile crossed his face.

"You don't know when to quit, do you, babe?"

25

MELODY

"I'll never quit," I answered, letting the door close behind me. "Not on you, no matter what you say. Because I love you, Connor."

"Yeah?" he challenged, trying to sound tough, but I heard the emotion crack through his voice. "What if I lose control and hurt you? Really hurt you. Would you still love me then?"

"Raz and Hunter won't let that happen." I crossed my arms. "So yes, I'll still love you even if you lose control and I'll try my damn hardest to get you any help you need."

He gave me a long, lingering look, his forest green eyes examining me from head to toe. "Have you been with them?"

I nodded.

"Both?"

Another nod.

He let out a heavy sigh and let his head fall back again as he shut the TV off.

"Does that bother you?" I asked in the resulting

silence.

"No," he answered. "Rather, the opposite. It gives me hope that we can still work, since you have them to balance me out. But," he shook his head, "I'm not worth it, babe. I'm just dead weight at this point. I'll drag y'all down so it's better to just cut me loose."

"I'm not doing that," I said, gritting my teeth so hard my jaw already ached. "I am tired of you beating yourself down over this shit, Connor. I love you. You love me. Let's be together. It's that simple."

"It's not, babe. And you know it." His hard stare bore through me. "I have to sell the trailer, and even then I'll still be so deep in the red, bill collectors will harass me for life. I can't perform without being in a world of pain. That pain is going to trigger worse and more vivid flashbacks. I am a *danger* to you, Melody. If you're in the wrong place at the wrong time, I could *literally* kill you. Your life is at risk by staying with me."

"I. Don't. Care," I answered, my vision blurring through the tears. "We'll find a way. I don't know how or when, but we'll figure this out, Connor. I would do anything for you. Can't you see that?"

"Why?" he demanded. "The country I fought for, and lost limbs for, had no problem discarding me after I returned home. My fiancee was happy to leave me for someone else. No one in my family could take me in because my disability was too inconvenient, plus I was another mouth to feed. Why do *you* give a fuck about me so much?"

"Because I know you would do the same for me," I cried, the tears spilling freely now. "If I pushed you away when I needed you, you'd make me come around to reason. I know you're doing this to try and protect me from yourself, but you don't need to! I have them to protect me." I shot my hand back toward the door. "But they won't need to either because I know the person you are, Connor. I know you would never hurt me…" I sniffed and wiped my nose, letting my tears fall freely to the tile floor. "You're only hurting me right now by pushing me away."

Only my sobs filled the room for several long moments. When I dared to look up at Connor, the pain on his face brought a fresh wave of tears to the surface.

"Fuck… Come here, babe."

I ran to him, burying my face in his hospital gown, and sobbed openly, letting out everything that weighed on me for the past several days. I almost forgot how thick and strong his arms were until they encircled me. I almost forgot how I could truly hide in the safety of him.

"What am I gonna do, babe?" he murmured, stroking my hair with a soothing hand. "You may love me now, but what about later down the road when you inevitably hate me for being a useless piece of shit?"

"I could never hate you." My voice muffled through his shirt. "I don't care if you lose your arms, legs, or your mind. I am here for you because you were there for me."

"What about my dick?" Of course, he couldn't resist such a joke to try lightening the mood.

I looked up at him through puffy, bloodshot eyes. "Hunter and Raz still have theirs."

"Oh, right."

My head flopped back down on his chest, neither of us saying more. His hardheadedness pissed me off so much and I felt like I was running out of strength to argue. I didn't feel like I convinced him to stay, and he sure as shit didn't convince me to leave. So here we were, at a standstill. Neither one of us giving an inch, yet unable to resist this connection between us. His arms felt like heaven around me and the way he stroked my hair told me how much he missed this. Missed *us*.

"Doesn't this feel right?" I asked him, my voice raw. "Don't you just want to stay like this forever?"

"Of course I do," he muttered. "But I feel selfish to take all this love from you when you have two more deserving guys right outside the door."

"I fucking hate it when you talk like that," I snarled, lifting my head to glare at him. "If I deserve love, Connor, then so do you. I'm nothing. I'm nobody. And I found three of you that mean the world to me and you all make me better than what I was."

"Now you know that's not true." He stroked my face and lowered his voice to a whisper. "You're a shaman, maybe one of the last ones. The shifters need you. I need you too, but selfishly. They need you to survive."

"Just because some guy gave me a coin when I was a kid!" I screeched. "He could have passed it on to anybody."

"I don't believe that." Connor shook his head. "I think he saw something in you that was already there. The power he passed on just enhanced what you already had, Mel."

Exhausted, I laid my head back down again. Round and round in circles we went, never getting anywhere. We'd already argued for too long and the nurses would burst in at any minute to kick me out. Not even Razvan could distract them forever.

When I heard the door open behind me, I squeezed my eyes shut and clutched Connor's hospital gown in my fists. They wouldn't take me away from him. I'd hold on for as long as I could. I was *not* saying goodbye. I'd show them all just how stubborn I could be.

"Doc." Connor's voice registered surprise as he laid a hand on my back. "Something up?"

"Ah, hello, Connor. And miss Melody. I hope I'm not disturbing you."

Quickly wiping my face, I looked over my shoulder to see Dr. Harman looking unkempt but happy. His shirt was wrinkled and his hair stuck out in all directions like he'd been sleeping at a desk or something, but the smile on his face shone like the sun.

"I'm sorry, Doctor." I cleared my throat, standing straight up. "I know visitors aren't allowed this late, but I—"

"Oh, no worries!" He held up a hand. "I have great news and came to deliver it straight away. It's good that you're here."

"What is it?" Connor's eyes narrowed, brows furrowing in skepticism.

"I got a call back from an old colleague of mine who is eager to meet you," the doctor bounced excitedly on his feet. "He's a brilliant guy running a non-profit for disabled vets much like yourself. He'll fit you with brand new prosthetics featuring the latest technology. They also have counselors specializing in combat PTSD, resources for job placement, housing, and the like."

My heart lifted as the room fell silent. Dr. Harman and I looked at Connor expectantly, who still wore a mask of distrust on his face.

"What's the catch?" he muttered.

"The only catch," the doctor inhaled, "is that he's in Georgia."

"Okay, but what's all this gonna cost?"

"Connor," the doctor laughed. "It's a non-profit organization! There is no cost to you."

"That's great!" I squealed, squeezing Connor's hand, but he still looked unconvinced.

"That's all good, but after I get the hell out of here, I still can't afford to make it to Georgia."

"They have programs for covering medical expenses, too. But Connor, listen." He approached the bedside, making sure to look directly at him. "I told my colleague a bit about you and he's very personally interested in helping you. I don't think he'll have any issue covering costs or whatever else you need."

Connor eyed him suspiciously. "Why? What's he so interested in me for?"

"I'm not sure myself but when I told him your full name and a bit about your condition, he essentially said he would move mountains to get you the care you need."

Connor's eyes flickered away from him, focusing on nothing as he absorbed this new information like a sponge. Or, as I knew, stubbornly trying to find a reason to refuse.

"It's a lot to process, so I'll leave you two alone to discuss it," Dr. Harman smiled, looking at both of us. "If you say yes to this, Connor, we'll be happy to discharge you in the morning and send you on your way."

"What do you think?" I asked once the doctor left, giving him a teasing poke on the shoulder. "You're all out of excuses now."

Connor sighed, knowing I was right. "It sounds too

good to be true," he muttered, the best excuse he could give.

"Well, getting there won't be easy. We still have to get all the way to fucking Georgia."

"We?" he lifted an eyebrow.

"Well, yeah. There's no way I'm *not* coming with you." I crossed my arms, and he knew better than to argue. "I'm sure Raz would be along for the ride. Hunter and the kids too, maybe."

"Why's this guy so interested in me, though?" he wondered aloud. "Maybe he has a sick double-amputee fetish and the non-profit is just a front for his creepy dungeon."

"Connor," I groaned, dropping my forehead to my hand.

"It's possible, babe."

"But highly unlikely." I pinched my brow. "Maybe it's a military connection? He could have worked with you or someone you knew?"

"Also not very likely." To my surprise, he grabbed my arm and pulled me close. His mouth crashed down to mine before I had a moment to breathe, but in that instant, he was the air I needed. "You did this," he murmured against my mouth.

"What?"

"You. It's always you. The moment I'm about to say fuck it all and go off the deep end, you pull me back. And you show me it's worth it to keep going." He stroked his thumb against my cheek, the dense forest of his eyes pulling me in. "To the shifters, you may be a shaman, but to me, you're an angel."

My heart crashing into my ribs, I brought my hand up

to his. "Does this mean you're not leaving me?"

"I know I'm a fucking idiot, but I'd be an even bigger idiot to do that." He lowered his forehead to mine. "I keep putting you through hell babe, and I don't know how you can stand it."

"Because I know it's not the real you doing that. It's what's been done to you." I wrapped my hands around the back of his broad neck. "And if this guy in Georgia can help you fight through that hell and bring out more of the real you, how could I not stick around for that?"

"God fucking damn it, babe. I love you so much."

He pulled me against him so tightly, I climbed into his hospital bed to reach him. We barely fit in the narrow space together, but that didn't matter. He wrapped me up in him, kissing me like it was our last day together, even though this was just the start of something new.

"I'm going to be a cranky bastard," he warned me between kisses. "I'm going to be pissed off and probably an asshole. I'll never be perfect but I swear to God, I'll try my best every day for you."

"I know you will," I told him. "You already do. Sometimes you push yourself and try too much." I gazed up at him. "Remember to be kind to yourself, too. Don't get upset if something isn't working. Try to love yourself as much as you love me."

"That will never happen," he laughed. "But I'll work on keeping my damn ego in check and letting shit go."

"That's all I want." I rested my hand over his heart, finally relaxing against him. "So we're heading to Georgia, then?"

"Guess so." He planted a kiss on my forehead. "Yee fuckin' haw."

EPILOGUE
MELODY

"What the fuck is up with Hunter?"

"I don't know," I admitted, stacking the last few boxes of supplies into Razvan's trailer. I shoved and tugged on a few things to make sure they were secure before closing the doors and latching them. Traveling light was apparently not in Raz's vocabulary.

Hunter begrudgingly agreed to come to Georgia with us, although he seemed he'd rather do anything else. He'd be driving Conner's RV since the doctor advised him not to use any prosthetics until he got fitted for his new ones.

He got discharged this morning, grumbling the whole time nurses pushed him in a wheelchair. Raz flew back to camp to bring his truck to the hospital, and Connor wasted no time hauling himself out of the wheelchair and into Raz's passenger seat.

"It's just temporary, babe," I reminded him, kissing his cheek. "Besides," I whispered breathily in his ear. "It might be fun sometimes."

"Naughty girl," Razvan chuckled delightedly, squeezing my thigh as he drove.

"We can use any regular chair for that," Connor grumbled, but I saw the smirk twitch on his lips.

"I dunno, man. Having wheels sounds like an extra bit of fun." Raz's eyes flashed excitedly at the road.

After getting packed up and hitting the road for a long journey ahead, I decided to ride in the RV with Hunter and Connor. Raz would be following us in his truck, hauling his own stuff behind him.

"Ride with me after we take a pit stop, *steluţa*," he growled, pinning me against the side of his trailer with a savage kiss that made my knees weak. "I can only go so many hours without seeing you."

"I have a feeling you'll drag me over here anyway," I teased, running my teeth along his ear. "Don't dragons like to kidnap maidens and hide them in their lairs or something?"

"If that's your fantasy, I can make it happen," he groaned, releasing me reluctantly before giving me a long look. "You gonna try talking to him?"

"I'm sure at some point, the boredom will get to me and I'll say something," I chewed my lip. "When that happens, Connor will back me up if there's a fight. But mostly, I just want to take a nap."

"A woman after my own heart," he chuckled, gazing down at me. "Have fun with them. I'll see you somewhere in Alabama."

My home state, not that I ever really had a home. We'd have to drive through on our way to Georgia, maybe even pass through Waterford, where I grew up. I thought about visiting my family and quickly shuddered with disgust. The further I stayed away from there, the better.

I climbed into Connor's RV, engine already running, to find him and Hunter talking in low voices in the front seats. They stopped talking the moment I got inside. I rolled my eyes and plopped down on the bed. Whatever. We'd have days to hash out whatever was going on.

The winding road put me to sleep immediately, but I was wide awake in another place, another body.

THE HUMANS GAVE me some shitty, half-rotten roadkill to eat for the first time in days. I still tore into it like it was a fresh, warm kill. How long had it been since I felt the satisfaction of hunting? Of bringing down prey and taking my fill? It felt like lifetimes ago.

When I finished the shitty meal, I pretended to be sedated when the human came to check the locks on my cage. He thought it would be funny to pull on my tail.

"Aaargh! Oh fuck, oh God!"

His human eyes only registered an orange blur as I swiped at him, claws outstretched and ready. I moved faster since losing so much weight, but even without the strength I once had, my claws tore through his soft human flesh like butter.

I only got his arm. He would eventually heal, but it didn't diminish the satisfaction of seeing his skin torn to ribbons, blood quickly staining his clothes a dark red. My cage was filthy, and I hoped he'd get an infection.

"Stupid fucking cat!" He grabbed a nearby cattle prod

with his good arm and stuck it through the bars, the electric end sparking menacingly.

I gave him a toothy grin, even while growling through the pain of the zaps. His dominant arm was the one I injured, so he missed shocking me several times. Throwing the tool down and stomping away, I knew he'd return with the other human. The one who liked to pump me full of drugs. He'd probably give me the nerve injection again, to make my pain worse.

Oh well. It was worth it.

Hello?

I snarled in surprise. The voice rang through my head so clearly, soft and feminine. I rubbed my cheek against the bars as a deep purr rumbled in my chest. Although it wasn't a physical touch, I felt the presence of someone warm, gentle, and caring.

My name is Melody. I'm a shaman. Do you know what that is?

A shaman? I echoed. I hadn't heard that word in years. Not since Lhosten came to visit my family when I was a child.

Yes, I do, I answered. *I can't believe there are any of you left.*

I'm just getting into my powers, Melody admitted. *I've seen through your eyes in my dreams. I want to help you. Where are you?*

I don't know, I told her. *I'm kept in a cage in a shipping container when they're not making me jump through fire. I've been shipped all over the country dozens of times.*

I'm traveling now and I think I'm getting closer to you, she said. *I feel your presence getting stronger.*

I hope that's true, I replied. *The longer they keep me here, the weaker I get. I've not been performing well enough and I think they'll dispose of me soon.*

I'll find you, she said, conviction in her voice. *I promise.*

THANK you so much for reading *Smoke and Mirrors!* Book 4 in the series, *Jump through Fire is available now!*

NEWSLETTER & READER GROUP

Never miss a book release, plus get three *free* short stories when you sign up for my newsletter!

Grab your freebies at:
  crystalashbooks.com/freebies

You can also join my reader group on Facebook to get updates and hang out with fellow readers.

Join Crystal's Coven at:
  facebook.com/groups/crystalscoven